ALL VISITORS ASHORE

"Combines a gritty naturalism with a poet's vision and an almost Proustian preoccupation with memory . . . fiction that is beautifully written"   JOHN MELLOR, *London Magazine*

"Auckland as never before in poetry or prose"
                                    SUSAN GRAHAM, *Herald*

"Stead makes it look so easy you don't realise till afterwards that very few people can put together such luminous sentences"
                                    IAN SHARP, *Sunday Star*

"It seems ironical that for sheer immediacy, for the annihilation of distance between writer and reader, we should have to turn to a novel located on the Auckland waterfront . . . for that intimacy and precision which most novelists seek and seldom find . . . An intricately clever and engaging novel"
                            NORMAN SHRAPNEL, *Guardian*

GW00391013

C. K. STEAD was Professor of English at the University of Auckland until 1986. He is known to students of literature as the author of *The New Poetic*, a study of Yeats, Eliot and the Georgian poets. He is the only New Zealand writer to have won the New Zealand Book Award for both poetry and fiction, which latter he has won twice for *All Visitors Ashore* and *The Singing Whakapapa*. He is a fellow of the Royal Society of Literature, and in 1984 he was awarded the C.B.E. for services to New Zealand literature. He lives in Auckland.

C. K. Stead

ALL VISITORS
ASHORE

THE HARVILL PRESS
LONDON

First published in 1984 by the Harvill Press in Great Britain
and by William Collins Publishers Ltd in New Zealand

This paperback edition first published in 2001 by
The Harvill Press, 2 Aztec Row, Berners Road, London N1 0PW

www.harvill.com

1 3 5 7 9 8 6 4 2

© C. K. Stead, 1984

C. K. Stead asserts the moral right to be identified as the author of this work

A CIP catalogue record for this book is available from the British Library

ISBN 1 86046 936 1

Printed and bound in Great Britain by Mackays of Chatham

To whom it may concern

ONE

The Dreamtime

Let's begin with the tea towel – it's hanging over a string and damp so the string curves downward under the sink bench and Melior Farbro, the old master, who is not so old, a little over fifty like the century itself and in good shape despite his limp and his endless complaints about corns, piles, tinea, peptic ulcers, migraine, bends down to dry his fingers on its brown checks. He has been making a salad and now he limps with it to the counter that separates his kitchen from his studio and puts it down in front of Curl Skidmore who is thirty years younger and hungry and likes salad and fresh fruit but doesn't think of them as food. Farbro squeezes a lemon over the salad and tosses it so oil and lemon mix through and Skidmore is watching Farbro's fingers which are long and broaden at the nails, spatulate, while all the time Farbro is talking and the sun is shining in and shining down on the garden beds out there where the lettuce and tomatoes and green peppers that are in the salad grew alongside the lettuces tomatoes and green peppers that are still growing. The sun is shining on red peppers drying on the peeling window sills and on sunflower heads bristling with black seeds you pluck out and chew for the oil and what it does for your corns, piles, tinea, peptic ulcers, migraine while Farbro is putting out cold smoked fish with the salad and telling Skidmore there's nothing a young man needs a woman for, nothing his pals can't provide and make it better, let's not go into details, and Skidmore is regretting that it's brown bread, healthy and rough and good for the bowels but with salad and fish he would have liked unhealthy white floury light warm doughy bread fresh from the bakery on the corner you can smell even down at the beach when the wind blows the

I

right way on a yeasty night and he has her against the retaining wall her skirt in his teeth to keep it from falling down over the business and her bush in his palm. Nothing, Farbro is saying, not noticing that the young Skidmore who has gone back a moment to the beach and the night and the easing of thighs this way and that against the slope of the retaining wall is shifting from buttock to buttock on the stool on the studio side of the counter and hand in pocket is making an adjustment. Farbro has put a plate in front of him, is putting cold potato salad beside green salad and he's saying he has some cold sausage – salami – if the fish isn't enough and then he's back to the subject of what boys can do for one another, thinking of himself as a young man and of little Kenny, tough little bugger, knowing everything right from the start and taking it all in his stride without ever a qualm or a tremor or a worry, and is that maybe what's holding up this lanky Skidmore whose hands move so daintily over his food (but nothing dainty about the quantities he's putting away) and he's saying yes, some salami would be nice. In Farbro's day it was 'the fear of God' they used to say they would 'put into you' to keep (he used to think) the pleasures of the prick out. So slicing the salami with little yelps of pain pretending it's a piece of himself he reaches over to push the pieces on to the plate of young Skidmore who is losing his sense of that yeasty beach scene and is now looking up and around. He takes in again the easel and the work bench and drawing board, the stretched canvases and sketches and water-colours, the pinned-over walls and the long shelf of art books and folios of prints, and the long strips of heavy paper, on which Farbro says his new work will be done, hanging over the arms of the canvas chair. Through the door and another door both open Skidmore catches sight of the green over-arched enclosure of the back garden filled with bird-sound and the faint clatter of the typewriter of Cecelia Skyways unseen in the garden hut writing her *Memoirs of a Railway Siding*. And Farbro taking a moment to look at this young visitor while the visitor is looking around him is thinking This lad has an eerie charm and he talks well and probably has talent but there are so many with talent and what becomes of them?

* * *

And now the tea towel with the brown checks is again heavy on the string, the string curving further towards the floor, the dishes washed and dried and put away, and Melior Farbro is seated in the canvas chair having thrown the long strips of heavy paper like a suit of clothes on a hanger across his day bed and moved the easel into a corner and guided Curl Skidmore to a comfortable chair. He has rolled himself a cigarette and passed the makings to Curl who is expertly following suit, keeping the paper moving at the tips of his ginger fingers, pinching the strands from either end after the last deft roll-and-lick-and-roll. The light passes from one to the other and there is the silence of the satisfied in-breath while they hold it there, letting the smoke hang a while in the lungs, pleasantly agitating, and with no sense in either of vast dark consequences to come, this being 1951 and it being the mark of manhood and the seal of friendship to exchange the poison weed and set it smoking down there inside you. Cecelia Skyways' railway words clattering on a distant surge of her typewriter flow a moment into the silence of the indrawn breath conjuring sidings, steam and the clank of joining wagons, and then Skidmore and Farbro breathe out and the pallid smoke, deprived of its best tars, flows forward in two greeting dissolving streams. Farbro is looking at the back of his hand held up against the light from the windows, turning his spatulate fingers this way and that, and already Curl knows from this sign that the old man is considering.

'You have intelligence,' Farbro says, 'and a good appetite, so there's nothing you can't do if you go about it in the right way.' There is a heavy stress on that phrase the right way and Curl Skidmore knows, half-knows, has picked up but won't let himself quite recognize it, won't do more than glance at it obliquely, that the right way for the old master doesn't mean Patagonia (he thinks of her as Pat) against the sea wall on a yeasty night. It might include a bit of that but only and always recognizing that cruising the loos and the docks for gentlemen partners is living dangerously but not half so dangerously as cruising where Farbro guesses Curl may be situated now on the borders of the vast bog of domesticity, the average, the norm,

3

mothers and fathers and kiddies and debts, no canvas or heavy paper or (as it would be in Skidmore's case) galley proofs draped over the camp bed, no clatter of the railway siding words of Cecelia Skyways flying up among the passion fruit and pawpaws, no art, because there is no art of the average, no art of the mean, of the mean in heart (Farbro is in full flow) and there is besides (he avers) the fact that all art is androgynous and you have the hands, my boy, you have the hands. Curl's eye is fixed on a cobweb in a cobwebby corner but he has shot down his flying hands, brought them home to base where they lie awkwardly on his lap playing dead with a bad grace. It is with a desperate honesty, feeling he's climbing a high stone wall, heaving himself over it, that he brings out the fact (his eye still on that broken web stirring in a breeze from the open windows) that he has a girl, that she has moved in with him in his glassed-in verandah down on the beach, that her name is Patagonia (he calls her Pat), that she would like to meet Farbro because she is a painter, a student of art.

Silence, while the old man considers the back of his hand, his spatulate fingers turned this way and that, and then a formal invitation like a card on a tray. Next time Curl comes he must bring her.

Curl Skidmore walks dejected at the water's edge, barefoot on the wet sand that the small waves slide over. He doesn't know why he is dejected. It is summer, the sun is shining, the Gulf is blue and calm, there is a sense of space, the sea spreading away to and around the islands of the Gulf and one big ship going out past Rangitoto through the immense wide gateway to the world. He walks, hands behind his back, his stomach comfortably full of Farbro's lunch, his head comfortably light with Farbro's wine, the sun feeling its way through his shirt to his shoulders, the sliding water cooling his feet with a hissing sound over the coarse-grained yellow-orange sand, full of some vague yearning that might be for anything – God, Fame, Nirvana, Great Love, Extinction – and only (Skidmore thinks in the wisdom of his twenty-one years) a fool would tell you that one of these words with a capital letter fitted the feeling better than another, or that it ought to be just one of them, but the world is full of fools and nothing is more entrapping, more enticing, than a word with a capital letter and there is a triple-fool in Skidmore (he knows this too) who can dispense with God and Nirvana but would like Fame, Great Love and Extinction all together and in equal measure. The beach is deserted, the mothers are shopping the fathers are at work the children haven't been let out of school and there is only Skidmore and a capering dot that grows as the distance between them diminishes and becomes a dog, a brown-black dog, a bedraggled mongrel spaniel which chases sticks for Skidmore out into the calm water and returns, shaking itself on the sand, and grips the stick more tightly and growls and twists when Skidmore tries to take it and in a moment releases it and as it flies from his hand turning and seeming to float against the blue sky before falling to the gently rising water, runs yapping and bounding and swimming to retrieve it. So it is out of a flurry of sand and dog and stick and water that Curl looks up to see a couple walking hand in hand at the water's edge and as they near him and hesitate and turn away and turn back he registers that it is Felice, the wife of Nathan Stockman the violinist, and that the little hand of Felice (who is a soprano) is resting in the large red hand of their cook. Not that they have a cook as people have cooks in novels or in history or in England, but the beautiful house of Nathan and Felice Stockman designed by Nathan's architect brother among the pohutukawa trees and looking over rock and water at the end of the beach has been turned into a restaurant where, it is advertised, you can eat and look out to sea and listen to 'Nathan and his Gipsy Violin'; and since every restaurant of quality needs not so much a cook as a chef it is in fact (correcting the fact) in the hand of their chef that the tiny hand of a potential Mimi called Felice is at present unfrozen and indeed entirely unthawed. And Skidmore thinks it's odd they should turn away like that and he feels (wrestling with one end of the stick while the spaniel whose name is Rosh growls and hangs on grimly to the other) something like disappointment thinking of Felice's high pure notes floating out through the branches of the moon-filled pohutukawas and of Felice's big

5

swelling soprano bosom and of her white neck and her round red mouth moulding the notes. Not that he thinks of her very precisely (throwing the stick so it turns end over end against the sky while the spaniel skitters to the water) because she is at least twenty-five and perhaps more and there is something (he suspects so) motherly about the way she pats his shoulder and his bottom and pinches his cheek when they meet. They are walking away now, she and the cook, no longer hand in hand. Perhaps he's her brother, Curl thinks, making a dash at the spaniel as it comes out of the sea.

Melior Farbro rests on his hoe between the bean rows his mind running between the skinny Skidmore who ate so much and talked more and the memory of Kenny as a young man eating very little and talking less but always observing – the two of them so different Farbro wonders why they should go together in his mind. He twists the hoe so the brown volcanic soil that would blow away in summer dust if it were not enriched with compost parts and crumbles around the bean stalks and begins yet again to compose a letter to Kenny he won't write warning him that the Government means business this time, he's sure of it, and that Kenny should stay out of it, not take part in executive decisions because the police will be looking for anyone well up in the union they can bring any sort of charge against and that if Kenny goes cruising just once while the heat is on . . .

But of course he won't write it because Kenny would think it was the old jealousy rising again trying to keep him off the streets, trying to make him all Farbro's own – and would that, Farbro asks himself, be entirely untrue? Leaning on his hoe again he listens to the bird notes which he can't identify but which have the feel of the warmth of the day about them, and then he notices that there is no sound from the hut, Cecelia has finished her stint for the day, her typewriter is silent. And as he looks towards the hut the door opens and a Botticelli face enhaloed by ginger-gold curls through which the sunlight for a moment astonishingly strikes looks out, sees itself looked at from the bean rows and with a gasping-in of breath withdraws

6

again. Silence but for the bird calls until slowly the door moves, inches open again and slowly the bright head puts itself forth and a voice as sweet and clear and remote from this world as the heavenly head it issues from says, 'It's you Melior' (Who else? he thinks, smiling however), adding that she thinks she will make a cup of tea and would he like one? He nods, yes he would like one, and she gathers herself at the still only half-open doorway and then in a flash she is down the two steps into open ground that might be raked with machine-gun fire and crisscrossed with mine-fields, across it and up the three steps into Farbro's house, banging the door behind her.

At the concrete steps that lead up to the white gate Curl Skidmore stops, his feet sinking in the dry sand, and throws the stick. The brown-black spaniel who is called Rosh bounds a few yards and stops. Skidmore is darting up the steps. Rosh follows but the gate snaps shut. Skidmore looks over it and down into brown doggy eyes. The docked tail moves faintly from left to right, enquiring. Skidmore says No, trying to sound as if he means it, and the ears go down and the tail stops moving. No animal, Skidmore thinks, has a right to look so human and so entirely deserving. As he goes along the side of the glassed-in verandah he admires the look of the island matting he has nailed over the weatherboards inside, and Pat's painting of them, him and her, cubed into the angles of the sea wall but unmistakably and sexually spliced together, which hangs over the matting. She is not in the verandah room nor in the little kitchen which is also the verandah, partitioned. She is in the bedroom which opens off the kitchen and which is just big enough to hold the double bed she is lying on and the wardrobe with the mirror on its door and the chest of drawers with the mirror above it. And because the mirrors are exactly propped and angled and because she is lying in exactly that place on the bed and because she hasn't jumped up to greet him and thrown her arms around his neck or punched him on the arm or kneed him in the balls he knows she has been waiting for him to come home and that she is wanting to play the Game. Her eyes you would say were shut but he knows they are slits and from that angle she can see her mirror, the one on the wardrobe door propped open to suit her, and that when he is in position he will be able to see his mirror, the one over the chest of drawers. So he plays his part now, tiptoeing into the room and finding her asleep, someone he has never seen before whose name (for all he knows) might be Patagonia or Aorewa or de Thierry or Bennett and whose wavy black hair is spread over the white pillow and whose ancestry might be Maori or French or (as it is in fact if the fact were only known to this unknown intruder skirting the bed's edge loosening his belt) something of both. He checks the window and seeing no one in the dazzling white yard with the cabbage tree at its centre he draws the blind leaving the sash window up. Then slowly quietly he returns to the girl on the bed who shows no sign of knowing he's there. Her skirt is over her knees and he lifts it a little and a little more revealing a smooth olive thigh and a little more revealing more of the firm curving smooth olive thigh and a little further revealing thin pants through which the dark bush darkly looks, and below which the thin pale transparent cloth is wrinkled and absorbed into the bulges and folds and declivities of a vulvar landscape – a sight so palpable even without touch he at once removes his trousers and underpants to make room for the occurrence that troubled him last at Melior Farbro's board . . .

So that's how it was you remember Aorewa, and as I look up from my leather-topped desk to the stuccoed wall and the clerestory light that was done in imitation of Nathan's house along the beach I can see two of Farbro's cartoon series (two of the best of those that survived) and beyond them on the wood-panelled wall that runs off at right-angles there's my early de Thierry, derivative but full of promise the experts say, and it was called the Game, you pretended to be asleep and I pretended to be a stranger and I removed my clothes and your clothes and you watched in your mirror and I in mine (as the hymn used to say). It was your favourite wasn't it, Patagonia? Why the silence? Are you refusing to answer?

Since this is going on inside your head Curlyboy, it's up to you whether I answer or not.

Curlyboy. I'd forgotten you called me that. And Earlybird. They were both in that letter . . . But we'll come to that. Yes, I require an answer.

I don't remember.

You don't remember the Game?

No.

The mirrors?

Vaguely.

We had a mirror each. It was the slowness that counted. Inching in you called it.

Eighthofaninching . . .

So you remember. It took a long time – the longer the better. And it took control. (Both senses!) Just one entry.

No I don't want to hear about it. I don't remember . . .

You do, Aorewa.

It – I mean the Game – it was what Cecelia Skyways would have called a Zen exercise . . .

The disastrous Dawn!

You could feel it approaching in me and I could feel it in you – the climax – from a long way off. We were so perfectly attuned . . .

'It is tone that makes music.'

The school motto! You remember that too.

May I go now?

Not yet. I want you with me.

Impossible.

I mean back in 1951.

Any particular location?

Still Takapuna but up the ridge again, right through Hurstmere Road shopping centre and Halls Corner and away along the . . . And off to the . . . And around the . . .

You mean back to Farbro's studio.

Yes. Hold tight . . .

Kenny, old boy (Farbro writes in his clear black script) I was thinking of you just now hoeing the beans and it must be time I dropped you a note. I was pleased to see you got elected to the union executive but I wish it wasn't that union or not that union at this time because Sid Holland means business, I can feel he's going to crack down, knowing that's what the public wants, and some of you boys will be in the firing line. What is it has gone wrong with the place, already I'm looking back on the Slump as the good times and I don't think it's just me who feels that is it? Of course they were good times for you and me and I still remember our gardening jobs in Remuera and even the days when we didn't manage to get a bob together for one square meal between us seem good when you look back on them. You know I'd like to see you and have a good talk and if there's trouble of any sort and you feel for any reason you want to lie low there's always a bed for you here. Not in the hut but I'm always comfortable on the day bed in the studio and the bedroom's all yours. Not the hut because I've got a sort of lodger – it's hard to explain about her (yes, old boy, it's a she – I wish I thought I'd made you jealous for a moment there but I know it's no such luck for me). She's a little tyke girl, a real sweetheart who spent as far as I can get it out of her nearly six years training to be a nun and then decided she couldn't stick it or wanted to do something different. Anyway she ran off to her aunt's place which is quite near mine and the aunt introduced me because Cecelia (that's the ex-nun) wants to be a writer and the aunt knows me – she's a very enlightened lady who buys my pictures sometimes and we chat at the greengrocer's – and knows I have literary friends like Rex. It's hard to get the whole story because the girl is so shy, frightened too (I don't know how she got up steam to make a break for it) but anyway there she is, I offered her the hut and she accepted and now she's writing a book in there. Her hair has grown out since she got out of the nunnery (or whatever it was) and it's bright ginger-gold just like a bush all around her head. You'd like the look of her, she'd make you think of some of those lads who used to be your favourites and used to make me so jealous. I had a skinny youth here today (another would-be writer – the world's full of them) and he reminded me quite a lot of you although I don't need to add he didn't have anything like your special charm. Well, old pal, I'd better get on with it (my little ex-nun has just brought me a cuppa) so I'll be seeing you but remember what I said about Sid and be careful now you're on the executive – they'll be hot on your tail if they can, this Government, so don't go taking any of your old risks. Look after yourself, Kenny, because you know I don't get any less silly as I get older (fifty-one this year, same as the century – as always!) and that means your old friend still loves you, boy.

The white concrete yard was no longer dazzling, the sun sloping beyond the ridge had gone off all but the topmost points of the cabbage tree, the spaniel had gone from the gate, the gulls were silent, and across the yard in their little whitewashed two-roomed flat Jim and June could be seen packing. Curl Skidmore, half sitting and half lying sprawled across the table at the end of the glassed-in verandah looked alternately across the yard to watch Jim and June through their uncurtained windows bouncing on the lids of over-stuffed suitcases and tea-chests, and out to sea where a cargo ship was sailing down the Gulf along the shoreline of Rangitoto that was catching full-face the light of the declining sun. Out there across that spacious surface of the Gulf was the gateway to the world towards which the ship was sailing and in a day or so another would sail and in it would be Jim and June. Curl had never wanted to join the godwits but now at the thought of Jim who was going to learn bullfighting in Spain and of June who was going with him and of them both drinking from wine skins and listening to castanets and flamenco singing and eating spiced food and walking under the hot sun in crowds where nobody spoke a word you could understand, Curl felt stirrings of unrest. Around the side of the house he could hear in the stillness between the hesitant breaking of small waves the dragging left foot of Mrs Battle who owned the house and let the glassed-in verandah and the little two-roomed flat across the yard and now her best-foot-forward-left-foot-drag step was joined by her throttled and yet somehow projected articulation of his name: 'Gurr-l' (step, drag) 'Gurr-l' (step, drag) as she rounded the corner into the darkening yard that still pulsed its stored sun-heat upward into the purpling velvet sky. 'Gurr-l' (step, drag) – her eternal dressing-gown dragging at mottled ankles and pom-pommed feet. Jim and

June have stopped bouncing and are poised unsteady one on a tea-chest the other on a trunk, both on the edge of hysteria. Patagonia is craning forward at the sink bench to look down on the thinning grey hair but holding back so as not to be seen. 'Gurr-l' (step, drag) – and by now Skidmore is moving to the door, dragging not one of his feet like Mrs Battle but both. In the darkening yard she gives him a lemon from her tree and an egg from her son's fowl house ('For your breakfast,' she says, keeping up her pretence that he lives alone and that the sounds which come through the wall from his bedroom to hers are some kind of athletics) and they talk about the weather (*'phew!'*) and that dog loose on the beach ('I'll call the Council if he gets in here') and the new restaurant along the beach ('They say it's run by a gipsy') and has he heard the news because for sure Mr Holland's not going to let the harbour fill up with cargo while those lazy good-for-nothing communists spend all day fishing off the wharves. And while she runs on about the Watersiders and what Sid Holland is going to do to them Curl Skidmore, his eye on the deepening velvet of the heavens above the cabbage tree, discovers a hole in his right trouser pocket and inserting two fingers, then two fingers and a thumb, widens it, and with further finger-work subtle and unseen by the impassioned Mrs Battle, draws his cock from his underpants out and up until it is sitting in his pocket . . .

She has run her course now and is step-dragging back around the corner of the house and Curl goes to the open door of the little flat and tells June to get down off the tea-chest and come and discover what he's got in his pocket.

'Sentimental prick,' says Melior Farbro, reading over his letter to little Kenny. But he seals it up and addresses it care of Mrs Hinchinghorn.

Jim and June had stopped packing to watch the white ship going out past Rangitoto. At first the sun was on it and it shone brilliantly but then the shadow that was racing across the Gulf intercepted it and began to edge up the narrowing slope of Rangitoto towards the crater. In two days' time they would be sailing down that same stretch of water looking out to see if they could pick out Takapuna beach and Mrs Battle's house and the whitewashed outhouses around the courtyard – their flat facing Curl and Pat's verandah, the seaward side enclosed by the outhouse containing the bathroom and laundry shared by the four of them, and the little square completed by the steep slope behind the house. Would they be able to pick out the white gate at the top of the steps up from the beach, and the tamarisks blowing along the fence-line? Jim took out a packet of Capstan, lit two and handed one to June. She was sitting on the lid that was supposed to close over one of their tea-chests but despite her weight springing woollen things bulged out all around. He drew on his cigarette watching the shadow climb the even slope of Rangitoto as the sun went down somewhere behind the ridge at their back, thinking of the last time he'd left New Zealand, sixteen years old and freshly kicked out of school with just his fare and five pounds in his pocket from his father and the idea that there was adventure to be had or money to be made in Australia on the cattle stations shooting kangaroos and snakes and riding under the gum trees. One suitcase had been enough, more than enough, it had rattled. Now there had to be blankets and sheets and pots and pans and cutlery because June said you couldn't be sure what a furnished flat would mean in Spain and if they decided to live a while in London first they would need all the blankets they had to keep warm. Also warm clothes and clothes for dressing up on the ship and you had to work out what went into the Hold and what went into the Baggage Room marked 'Wanted on Voyage' and what went into your cabin . . .

Curl had come out into the yard, he was talking to Mrs Battle. The ship had gone, the last of the light was on the summit of Rangitoto, June was laughing listening to Mrs Battle and watching Curl shifting from one foot to the other staring up into the cabbage tree and fiddling in his pocket. Mrs Battle was talking about the strike threat down on the wharves and Jim wondered whether it would happen and if it did when and would it be within the next few days and if it was would passenger liners be affected or only cargo ships. The wharfies had been offered an extra fourpence ha'penny an hour that would bring them up to about nine pounds a week without overtime but they wanted something nearer to ten and that seemed fair enough but more than the wharfies wanted ten pounds a week Jim wanted to get out of New Zealand. He had been reading Hemingway and as much as he'd ever yearned for Australia and the Outback and dingoes and wallabies and kookaburras and the big stations and opal mines and Death in the desert Jim yearned now for the heavy breath of the wounded bull and the graze of its horn making a last lunge along his tight-trousered matador's thigh and he up on his toes making a clean job of it with a single thrust of his sword up and over the horns and deadly into the heart. Did matadors travel with women who crammed blankets and pots and pans into tea-chests and then sat on them to nail down the lid? One suitcase and five pounds in the pocket seemed a more likely start. But Jim and June were married, she had worn a white dress, he had worn a dark suit, and for two years they had both worked as clerks living on her wage and saving his and now they had their tickets, they were packing and in two days' time they would be sailing out there, north towards the equator.

Mrs Battle was dragging her way back towards the corner of the house and now Curl was at their door leaning in and telling June to come over and see what he had in his pocket. She jumped down and went to the door where he was standing side-on holding his pocket open and she pushed her hand into it and drew away with a squeal. Curl said there was something almost as good in the other pocket and he pulled out two pound notes. That was for tonight, he said. He'd booked a table for the four of them at Nathan Stockman's restaurant, it would be a flash farewell, it would be the last supper.

Blessed Virgin (wrote Cecelia Skyways) it will interest you to know we are having a Language Release here in Takapuna this summer or you might call it just a plague of the verbal squitters. Even my friend Melior says he's finding it hard to resist the impulse to put words into his paintings, and of course I am hard at my Railway Siding memoirs every morning. And today Melior had a visit from a young writer called Skidmore who

(Melior tells me) says he has two complete novels in his head. I looked at him through a gap in the curtains as he was leaving and I thought it was a nice head and that there might have been another novel or two tucked away inside his trousers as well. (I'm glad you enjoy a joke. I've always thought a woman in your position who lacked a sense of humour would be sunk.) It's getting dark and I'm writing by the light of a kerosene lantern because there's no electricity in this hut and I'm glad of that because the last place I was in my head was so electrified my hair still stands out all around it, a kind of halo that makes me feel akin to you, B.V., whenever I see your picture. I haven't told Melior about the electrification of my head, people take fright so easily, I've told him I was in a convent which is near enough to the same thing. You know as well as I do this is a man's world and a woman has to tell some little lies and some bloody whoppers to get by. But Melior is kind to me, he's a sort of woman-man anyway, and right now he's cooking over there, I can smell it wafting across among the pawpaws and tree tomatoes and lemons and pears and grapefruit. And while he cooks he has the radio on and there's something that might be Bach or Telemann something baroque or rococo with a flute and a violin and one of those twangling instruments that Caliban heard (I'm a lady Caliban, my isle is full of noises) and that music fills the shadows between the trees that usually fill me with fear. But I am attending to my Zen Master who inhabits a web just over the door and he instructs me not to draw back from my fears but to go forward into them, to become my fear because it's the division in me between self and self that is the cause. Last night I lay in bed with my door ajar and out there lay the shadows and I looked at the shadows and the shadows looked at me and neither of us moved and when I thought I was going to die because my breath had stopped Melior's door opened and shot a long shaft straight into the shadows killing a couple of the worst of them dead and then out came Melior with a torch and he worked his way here and there pointing the ray this way and that shooting holes in shadows to left and right only stopping now and then to pick a snail or a slug off the leaves of his vegetables. It's a strange life people lead in

15

the suburbs, B.V., and I enjoy watching them come and go at exactly the same time, they look so full of purpose. I've got quite out of the way during my years indoors of seeing how they live inside their lives like sausages inside a skin. Melior's section is enclosed by trees and overgrown hedges, just perfect for someone like myself who is full of fear but needs to look out, and my Zen Master in the web tells me to observe is good, to interpret bad, so I become (like Christopher Isherwood) a camera pointing out at the suburb from Melior's trees. But there's a lady across the road who has a camera, a real one, and another lady on this side of the road who has a dog, a spaniel I think, called Rosh, and the camera lady says it's the dog lady's dog who is fouling her front lawn while the dog lady denies it. So the camera lady plants herself last week in her garden shed with the door ajar and when the dog lady's dog comes to deposit his business on her grass she snaps him once, twice and then a third time in full crouch and with the offending matter in emerging stages and now she says (they argue outside Melior's hedge) she has sent copies to the Council and she wants the dog destroyed. Destroyed! Doesn't that word send shivers into you, Blessed Virgin, it's what they did to your Son and I think the camera lady would welcome it if dogs could be crucified but as it is she'll settle for the gas chamber. Melior is calling me to dinner and he has opened the door so there's a straight yellow path through the shadows and I shall fear no evil but as I write that my Zen Master from the web says Go forward Cecelia Skyways, look for no protection but become your fear.

Where are you now, Nathan Stockman, somewhere 'over there' leading an orchestra, occasional soloist and with your own quartet noted for its recordings of Beethoven and Bartok, how would you like them to know (or do you tell them and laugh?) about your restaurant and the advertisement for 'Nathan and his Gipsy Violin'? How you winced when you thought of your friends who said you ought to be in Wellington leading the National Orchestra and imagined them reading the sign and the advertisements! But Felice was firm, she wasn't going to Wellington. Who could sing (she wanted to know) in a town where the wind blew as long and hard as it does in Wellington? It was too depressing. So there you were putting all your Jewish melancholy (that was how you described it) into your playing of a Bach sonata and there hadn't been much all that evening of the jolly gipsy in your playing. The light was dim in the restaurant so you could see out to the Japanese lanterns among the pohutukawas and catch a glimpse of the long curve of the beach with light from the houses shining down on to the sand and now and then the lights of a ship going along the line of Rangitoto towards or away from the harbour entrance. There were only two couples at a table by the window, the other five who made up the total for the night had gone, but it wasn't the small number of customers that made you melancholy and it wasn't even the thought that you should be down there in Wellington at the National Orchestra's number one desk, it was something else that was very near to you but just outside your range of vision, a sinking you might have felt if, as hereditary receptacle of that Jewish melancholy, you had been somewhere in Europe ten years earlier and someone had inadvertently knocked a little louder than necessary on your door in the night. It was a certainty that the bottom was going to drop out of everything, the trap was about to be sprung, the noose was in place, the gas canisters were ready, the wagons were rolling (Hitler made the cattle trains run on time!) and it – the big threat – it wasn't in Wellington or across the harbour among the silent stalks of the wharf cranes pointing up at the night sky or even out there in the suburban street, it was right here in the room with you. You felt sick with it, sick with the fear and worst of all with not knowing what it was and as you felt it it went through your fingers to the strings and the bow and you registered that the young writer, Scamper, or Skinflint, from along the beach had detached himself from the three he was with, he was leaning back in his chair taking in your music, and for a moment seeing what you heard heard also by the young Skillsaw from along the beach you soared into an ecstasy that didn't leave the melancholy behind but took it with you into the upper reaches of the empyrean. And that, my God, you deplored it, it was absurd, your own veering intensities, and as a protest against them and to deflate yourself and young Skidmore too who was looking so dewy-eyed in his appreciation of what your fingers were doing you bounced almost without a break into the 'Flight of the Bumble Bee'.

Full of wine now and wavering together and apart and two steps forward and one step back as they make a steady nearly no-progress along the sand from the restaurant these four are Curl and Pat and Jim and June and to keep not entirely out of sight but at a comfortable distance all thought of departures bullfights goats guitars Curl is reciting and running together aloud and along the beach the endless long runnable lines that are stored in his head (together with two unwritten novels) offering up to the heavens and into the wind *It was my thirtieth year to heaven woke to my hearing from harbour and neighbour wood and the mussel-pooled and the heron-priested shore the morning beckon with call of seagull and rook and the knock of sailing boats on the net-webbed wall* – and as that runs its course turning as quickly and unhesitatingly as Nathan Stockman turned from the Bach to the Bumble Bee replacing soon-to-be double-dead Dylan with the unmanned Manley Hopkins of *this morning's minion kingdom of daylight's dauphin dapple dawn-drawn falcon in his riding of the rolling-level-underneath-him-steady air*.

A breeze is coming across the Gulf making the warm night strangely chill as they pause at the gate under the blowing feathery tamarisks to say goodnight and to go to their separate flats that face one another across the moon-white courtyard with the spiky cabbage tree at its centre. And it is Pat now (Patagonia de Thierry Aorewa Bennett, as she sometimes says to the night, telling the moon her name) who thinks He is so remarkable with his head full of poems that unfold like scrolls and with two whole novels just waiting to be unwound and with that brilliant sensitive ferret face. He is her mystery-man and her brilliant-future-man and her lover-man and her child-man with a little of the husband too for formal occasions and even sometimes something like a father – one kind of father – for doing arithmetic and warding off ghosts. But tonight she wants to take with her into the big double bed the best of all Curl Skidmores which is not the real one but her idea of him, that golden boy of whom the horny intractable reality is only a drunken gabby and imperfect shadow. So Curl pawing at her in the dark, feeling for buttons and loops and openings, finds himself in his wine-haze pushed down on the divan under the verandah room's matting while the elusive Aorewa de Thierry, artist of the future with the Tuhoe-Parisian past, not for the first time but no less obscure to him in her motivations retires alone and smiling to their bedroom and locks the door.

Nathan Stockman lies very still looking through the clerestory glass angled under the roof to the upper branches of the pohutukawas stirring slightly against the starlit sky. He's tired but he can't sleep and he doesn't know whether Felice who lies beside him is asleep or only pretending to be. Lying there it has come to him, he knows, feels sure he knows, what has caused it – that nameless fear. It's that Felice is having an affair with that young Skidmore the writer from along the beach. Nathan wants to wake her now, if she's asleep, to challenge her, tell her he knows. But at the same time that he's certain, and feeling sick with the certainty, he knows he hasn't anything like proof, she will deny it, he might believe her denial and he doesn't want to believe it, because although the pain of knowing is so bad it's not as bad as the pain of not-knowing . . .

It seems to Nathan that he is wide awake, he won't sleep, must lie there unrelaxed all night torturing himself with his new knowledge and for a long time he does lie staring up through the arms of the pohutukawas into the infinite and uncomforting spaces between the stars. But at last Felice who has been lying waiting, staring into those same empty spaces, hears unmistakably the change in his breathing, the steady regular faint whistle of his breath that signifies he is asleep.

Melior Farbro turning his book face down on the table beside his bed reaches over to switch off the light. The two black cats at his feet, Agatha and Christie, stir and settle. He has listened out as the last bus from the last ferry has gone by, waiting as he does most nights for the footsteps of little Kenny that used to come from it and one of these days, when Kenny has had enough of freedom, Melior thinks might come again. Looking out into the back garden he sees Cecelia's lantern in the hut turned down and then extinguished. And in her hut with the door again bravely ajar Cecelia says – tries to say aloud so the shadows will hear but her voice shakes down to a whisper – goodnight to the Zen Master, and goodnight to the Blessed Virgin.

Unable to sleep under the blanket on the divan below Patagonia's cubist painting of lovers against a sea wall Curl Skidmore lies listening to the sound of the sea which has changed with the wind from a steady breaking of small waves interspersed with a rustling of shells to what is now a general unpatterned uninsistent agitation as of the chattering of a crowd in the dark. He tries to centre his mind on that sound, on its rises and falls, so sleep will come to him but it's no use. He wants Pat but he doesn't dare break in on the dream in which she's locked with her ideal unreal perfect and eternal Curl Skidmore to whom he, the real thing, the dinkum oil, Urlich Amrose Skidmore, known to his family and friends as Early (though he's usually late) and more recently as Curl (though his hair is as waveless as a dam in summer) bears some but insufficient resemblance.

He gets up from the divan and goes out into the yard where the long points of the cabbage tree clatter quietly against one another in the breeze. No sound from Jim and June. They are sleeping, dreaming Andalusian or Catalan dreams. He walks down to the beach breathing the beautiful fresh shellfish-and-seaweed smell that blows from the reef. Out there is the sprawling dark dreaming shape of Rangitoto, a beacon flashing from its western extremity. Under the pohutukawas around Nathan Stockman's restaurant he stops. Two figures have come out into the darkness, one small and fluffy, the other heavily built, and of course he remembers now as he watches them through the trees, sees them pushing two suitcases behind the bucket seats of the open MG and driving away without lights –

the sight of them on the beach that afternoon. It is Felice and
the chef and they appear to be running away.

TWO

Speech Balloons

Auckland is a harbour town, a town of two harbours, at the nether end of the world, and 1951 (properly counted) is the first year of the second half of the twentieth century. There are planes in the air, even passenger planes, but still people who travel do it by sea moving with the cargoes and like God upon the face of the waters. The ships come and go, they are our carriers and links, our assurance that our spacious and beautiful confinement though solitary is not absolute. They link us with 'Home', if there is somewhere far away we can think of as Home, or with our Catalan and Andalusian dreams. In 1951 the trams run to and fro across the Auckland isthmus all the way from the wharves at the bottom of Queen Street to the wharves at Onehunga. Everyone knows that the Waitemata harbour is the city port where all the big shipping arrives and departs and that the Manukau harbour on the west coast takes only coastal shipping because the sand bar across its entrance makes it dangerous for vessels with deeper draughts. And then to and fro across the Waitemata harbour threading among the shipping anchored in the stream go the ferries to the North Shore, to Devonport, Stanley Bay, Northcote and Birkenhead, and from the wharves on that side the buses run to the beach suburbs on the Hauraki Gulf – Cheltenham, Narrow Neck, Takapuna, Milford and beyond. There is talk of a harbour bridge and of taller buildings in Queen Street and of new methods with cargo and of huge airliners and airfreight but this is only the first year of the second half of the twentieth century – all that is to come and meanwhile Auckland still looks like a South Seas port with a predominance of wooden buildings and wooden wharf piles. At the ends of the wharves – or so you will hear it said – sit men in felt hats with fishing lines dropped down into the green harbour water. These are wharfies at work and that is why the cargo moves so slowly and there are ships in the stream through which the ferries have to thread their way. The wharfies are a tight strong union who elect tough men to speak for them. These spokesmen (you will hear it said) are communists or sympathetic to communism and in Korea in this first year of the second half of the twentieth century we are fighting communism and if we fight communism in Korea and communism in the unions (so goes the prevailing logic) it is the same fight and in both America is our ally. Our Prime Minister Sidney George Holland known to the fishermen in felt hats as the Senator for Fendalton has just come back from Washington where he has been reported as promising 'every fibre of his being' (not much fibre there, the fishermen say) in support of America and where he has said, 'Tell me what else I can do and I will do it.' Now he is going to do it and everyone knows he is going to do it, because the wharfies have cut themselves off from the Federation of Labour and they are demanding five shillings and twopence an hour (but everyone knows they would settle for four and tenpence ha'penny) and the ship-owners have offered four and sevenpence ha'penny and now the wharfies are saying they won't work overtime and that's where things stand as the wharfies gather at the Trades Hall in Hobson Street under the huge painted Vicks advertisement showing the head of a haggard old man swathed in blankets and with a handkerchief up to his mouth coughing his heart out.

The cabin was tiny, just two bunks a washbasin and mirror and a few narrow cupboards, but it had a porthole. It was close to the water so mostly the porthole would be clamped shut and in rough weather the sea would wash over it. But perhaps in the tropics, Jim thought, when the weather was hot and calm and people would be sleeping up on deck to keep cool, he and June would be able to sleep down here with it open – and as he said this he and June and Curl and Pat sitting in a row on the bottom bunk turned their eyes right and sat silent each of them imagining the rustle of the water of the middle latitudes swishing by out there while the big ship rushed them north where five weeks away London lay at the very centre of the world. The second call came over the speakers, All Visitors Ashore, and they got up to say their goodbyes again, embracing one another, saying (without quite believing it) that they would meet up in a year or two in Madrid or Barcelona or somewhere in the Balearic Islands, probably Majorca, where you could live on next to nothing and where Pat could paint cubist goats and cactuses and Curl could write one of the novels that were scrolled away inside his clever head.

'And bring your magic pocket,' June called down to him from the promenade deck as he and Pat made their way down the gangplank to the wharf. It was early evening, the sun was going and would be gone before the ship. On the wharf the crowd pressed together craning up to find their loved ones or relatives or friends among the passengers crowding the rails. There they were, Curl picked them out, Jim and June had found a place on the upper deck now under the second lifeboat. The streamers flew back and forth with shouts and promises and good wishes and then when everyone was standing ready waiting for the ship to cast off a huge mobile crane which had been loading the last of the cargo into the after hold began to lumber on its iron rails that ran between the ship and the platform on which the farewelling crowd was assembled. There were cries of disappointment as the iron monster slowly rolled the full length of the ship gathering to itself and taking away with it to the far end of the wharf every streamer, every one of those paper umbilicals stretching from ship to shore. Bedecked in them, it went on its way. There was a pause, a subsidence in the shouting and laughter, and then the streamers began to fly again, all colours, twisting and running out this way and that until the whole criss-cross maze was recreated and each person aboard held again a link with someone ashore. Now the funnel sounded long and loud, not so much a hoot as a rumble, so deep and vibrant the buildings of the central city seemed to quiver against the pallor of the western sky, and although the sun was gone behind the Waitakeres the sound drove the pigeons up from the ferry building for a final two circuits before dark. The tugs were in position, the ropes were cast, Jim and June were shouting and signalling their last messages but what they were saying it was impossible to be sure. And now the big ship which had seemed as solid and immovable as the shore, as if it was not afloat at all but sitting firmly on the harbour bottom, was seen to be moving. With surprising speed the gap widened, the streamers ran out, stretched, tightened, and one by one broke and fell fluttering to the water. The shouts grew more frantic yet fainter as the ship retreated and began to be turned about by the tugs and at the same time in the gathering darkness its lights shone out and from its loudspeakers came 'Anchors Aweigh' and 'Now is the Hour'. Already the faces lining the decks had merged into an agitated blur and as the ship turned its bow towards North Head they ceased to be individuals, they were not even a crowd, it was a big liner out there, a single beautiful remote and magical 'vessel', or (if you preferred to see it that way) just another ship, and perhaps the last for a while, leaving the Port of Auckland. Pat was crying. Curl tugged at her sleeve. It was time to go to Somervell's for a cup of coffee. Jim and June were gone (you could say it now) 'overseas'.

And the old man in the Vicks advertisement holds his coughing long enough to hear:

'. . . in the absence of our Chairman it's my job to tell you – the law requires me under these emergency regulations to tell you that the law requires you under the same emergency regulations to go back to work as directed by the Government. That's right, mates. That's how it is. And remember by work is meant not the forty hours we've offered to do but that and just as much overtime in addition as our employers the shipowners think is a good idea. If they want us to work eighty hours that's our duty under the law and if we refuse it's a strike. If you keel over that's probably a strike too. I'm not sure what happens if they want us to work more hours than there are in the week. I imagine it will have to be tested in the courts . . .'

And the old man in the Vicks advertisement laughs along with the rest of them and that sets him coughing again.

*   *   *

25

Two prows each with a lantern, two wheelhouses, two screws, front and rear, two decks, upper and lower, all wood, grinding now against the wooden piles because the skipper hasn't made his run quite straight. This is the ferry *Toroa*, over from Northcote, and these are its passengers clustered amidships waiting for the gangway to grind down and bounce on the deck (upper because the tide is low), and the younger males, the fitforactiveservice ones, lining the rails ready to jump before the gangway is down. And this is the Auckland ferry building, brown brick in Georgian style with pigeons which in daylight fly out from the tower at the quarters, regular as clockwork, but are now squabbling on their ledges for sleeping space. And these are the thick ropes creaking and slipping and tightening around the bollards and this is the bosun with the whistle between his teeth while he eases the ropes through, and these are the pistons like iron elbows you can see down in the engine room from the lower deck, going half astern as the ferry eases in and squares against the piles. And there go the fitfor-activeservice ones, making their jumps ashore, and here is the gangway grinding down and thudding on the deck and the 'midships crowd clattering over its lattice flooring. And this, holding back to left and to right while the passengers push ashore to the ticket barrier, is the crowd waiting to board for the return. And these two, hand in hand among the crowd waiting, are Pat and Curl, and this wild-eyed anxious one standing apart and unseen searching the faces as they come ashore is Nathan Stockman whose restaurant has closed and whose gipsy violin is silent. Now the North Shore passengers are all ashore and the waiting crowd moves aboard and Curl and Pat move with it over the gangway on to the upper deck and then down the stairway to the lower where they sit on a wooden bench looking into the darkness under the wharves that in daylight would show green water and green shafts of light.

It is a quick turnaround, *Toroa* is running behind schedule, and now the skipper has moved to the forward wheelhouse, prow is stern, stern is prow, gangway is hauled up, ropes unwind, bosun's whistle blasts, pistons move, screw that drove draws, screw that drew drives.

This rusted hull they are running the length of is a cargo ship over which wharf cranes hang idle in darkness, and now they are past it and this is open harbour reflecting the still night and the wharf lights in straggling lines across its surface. And this is Nathan Stockman coming down the stairway, making his way along the outside deck staring into faces as he passes. And this is Curl Skidmore and this is Pat Bennett whose faces he stares into, and this is recognition and embarrassment on his part and on theirs, and this is silence between them, there is only the regular thrust of the pistons like iron elbows and the irregular scraping of the fireman's shovel from the engine room and the swish of water past the bows, while Nathan Stockman hesitates and half nods and doesn't speak and passes on looking compulsively into faces as he goes.

And the old man in the Vicks advertisement hears:

' . . . the *Herald*'s leading article this morning and you'll have seen the accompanying cartoon by Minhinnick. From these you will have learned that you're all slackers and bludgers, with no consciences and no brains, and that you've got faces to match. And you will have learned that I and your president and secretary and the National leaders of our union – all of us are either conscious conspirators or else we're dupes of a communist plot. You think you just want a living wage. You think we've been working to try and get it for you. Well your paper will have told you otherwise this morning, brothers. And if I should argue with what the *Herald* says, or write a pamphlet about it and have it distributed, I would be contravening the law. That's the kind of law we're dealing with. No newspaper is allowed to print anything I might say in support of what is now – according to the new definition in the Regulations – a strike. You think it's a lockout. No doubt you do, my friends, but the law says it's a strike and it's an offence to say otherwise.'

Ashore at Northcote and the waiting bus takes Curl and Pat (it takes Nathan Stockman too, but he sits apart, staring out into the night) past the studio where we began and where earlier in the day the painter Melior Farbro and the poet Rex Fairburn, each locked in his obsession of the moment, had conducted something like the following exchange:

Fairburn: . . . a poetry reading. Big one. Ron Mason, me, and this young Jim Baxter from the South Island. Town Hall Concert Chamber seemed the right sort of place . . .

Farbro: And then I recognized I hadn't done anything new for years. I'd painted – but nothing different . . .

Fairburn: Absolutely everything arranged . . .

Farbro: I'm in a rut. An illustrator . . .

Fairburn: And with just the three of us, time for some longer poems. I thought I'd try . . .

Farbro: Old wooden houses on back country roads. Good for the records, but . . .

Fairburn: It came right out of the blue. Official letterhead . . .

Farbro: Then I moved it into a sort of cubism. John Weeks helped . . .

Fairburn: Police sent me to the mayor's office, mayor's office sent me to police . . .

Farbro: Landscape. But these are human figures . . .

Fairburn: Refused us flat. No reading at the Concert Chamber as long as the Emergency . . .

Farbro: Something to do with the Emergency . . .

Fairburn: Hasn't felt like this since '37 . . .

Farbro: Never thought of myself as a political painter . . .

Fairburn: Tried the newspapers. They won't touch it . . .

Farbro: But they've started to *speak*. Talking pictures . . .

Fairburn: Maybe some kind of broadsheet . . .

Farbro: Put a yellow circle in the sky. Very rough, with rough edges . . .

Fairburn: They know about Mason's political allegiances . . .

Farbro: Thought 'You've ruined your picture . . .'

Fairburn: Don't suppose they know he was tossed out of the C.P. fifteen years ago for insubordination . . .

Farbro: Just painted into the circle 'Come down out of your airwaves' – very rough . . .

Fairburn: Young Baxter. His father wrote a book about being a conshie in the First World War . . .
Farbro: Seemed to hang there – well forward . . .
Fairburn: We've sent him his fare. Won't see that again . . .

And so on. But after Fairburn had left, Farbro gave some thought to the poet's half of the conversation and wrote:

Dear Rex,
About the Concert Chamber ban – of course you're right. Political reasons. But look here (in haste) possible solution: Did I mention Stockman gossip? Nathan's little lady off and away with cook (or cock?). That's Felice – the singer with the big ones. (Almost makes me wish I was the sort.) Restaurant closed, losses, debts. So the place is up for sale. NOW. You can't have Concert Chamber. Why not use Nathan's place for your reading? Good idea? 'Sbig enough for poetry-size crowd and priv. prop. If you like plan phone and I'll approach Nathan (needs delicate handling just now – distraught at loss of Bigones). OK? And here's another one fresh out from under my hat: there's a young Narcissus living down on the beach (Battle's old house – you know it?) who 'writes' (novel planned – two in fact) – a horror I suppose as they all are at that age but has talent. Has written a thing on (about) Takapuna Beach – dramatic-rhapsodic Dylanish stuff but pretty good. Why not give him 5–6 mins in the middle? – a rest from the big guns (maybe light relief?). Think he's worth it. Name Skidmore. Let me know about that too and I'll carry down the tidings. And thanks for advice re. speech balloons. Good to have positive response. Have gone on with them.

Cheers,

M. F.

PS My little lodger in the hut, Cecelia, ex-nun, watched you go. Declared you 'impressive' – 'nose like Words-worth's, voice like God' (her words). Quoted your

29

This stubborn beach whereon are tossed
White roses from the sea's green bough
Has never sheathed a Norman prow
Nor flinched beneath a Roman host.
(Neither it has you old prick! But lovely lines.)

Whereon forsooth,
Mel.

While Fairburn, after returning home to Devonport and giving some thought to what the painter had been trying to say, wrote:

Look Farb,
If that's the way the impulse takes you – cartoon figures, speech balloons – just follow it, boy. If it's painted it's a painting – let someone else decide whether it's art.

And glad to have your support for protest about cancellation of Concert Chamber booking.

All the best,
Fairb.

PS No doubt it's time for a change in your work but taihoa the modesty about achievement. You're part of the history already. Just looked at my three Farbros to date and they don't (if you follow).

Rex.

And the old man in the Vicks advertisement, drawing the blanket back from his ears, listens again:

'Well lads, it's a cold hard world. We feel cheered by one another's company in this hall but we go out of it as individual men. Most of you have families. The days ahead aren't bright. However angry you feel – and I know how you're going to vote, and I agree with that – just don't underestimate what it's going to be like to find yourselves defined by law as criminals, to have the police empowered to seize the funds and records of your union, to enter your homes without warrant, to prevent anyone from giving you anything – money, food, clothing – that might help your families through. There's no need for me . . .'

'So let's get on with the voting,' shouts the old man in the Vicks advertisement.

Getting down from the bus in Hurstmere Road that evening leaving poor Nathan Stockman staring into his own reflection in the window (he had another stop to go) do you remember how it was, Patagonia de Thierry Aorewa Bennett (I think of you as Pat) wherever you are after these thirty years since that first year of the second half of the twentieth century and I who went by the name of Urlich Ambrose Skidmore (you sometimes called me Early, sometimes Ambrosia) my fingers pressed to my brows as we went down the long steep drive among the houses all the way down to Mrs Battle's house on the beach and they are the same fingers now remembering (if fingers can be said to remember) at the typewriter on the leather-topped desk under the stuccoed wall and the clerestory light how I pretended to a headache, called it a migraine, not daring to tell you of my madness, how the bottom dropped out of my world so that I didn't know who I was although I could tell you my name age occupation height address the momma's name the father's and all the rest of it but I had crumbled to pieces inside myself and was nothing at all. Nathan could say, 'My wife has run away with another man,' and Cecelia Skyways could say, 'They locked me up and electrified my head,' and Melior could say, 'A threat hangs over me because of my sexual preferences,' and his friend Ken could say, 'They hound all of us in this union because they think we're communists,' and even you, Aorewa, when your gallic mood left you and you felt stirring inside you the restless blood of your Tuhoe forebears could say, 'They see the colour of my skin and hair and something about the nose and mouth and they begin to treat me in a special way as if I were a child or mentally deficient.' But there was nothing I could think to say (pressing these fingers to my forehead) except that I had a headache. And that was a lie. Who had a headache, if there was a headache about? No 'I' existed, there was only nothingness and fear. In a moment it was gone but there remained the horror as we went down into the little courtyard under the cabbage tree. Out there the Gulf was

31

empty, Jim and June's liner had gone, their flat was empty and our door was ajar and inside it when we turned on the light was a bag of Melior's tomatoes and a green pepper and a lettuce and one of those white cucumbers and a note saying:

Dear Curl,
Rex Fairburn's reading at Concert Chamber cancelled (Emergency Regs). Have written suggesting holding at Nathan Stockman's and keeping space for you to read Takapuna piece. (5–6 mins – OK?) Will be in touch when he replies.

Best,
M. F.

And you, dear de Thierry, you had me in a hammer-lock and threw me to the floor it pleased you so much that I might get a chance to read my Takapuna piece to an audience along with those three 'real' poets, and you wrestled me around the floor hitting me and kissing me and tearing off my clothes. We ran across the lawn in the darkness risking the observing of the all-seeing Mrs Battle or of her son Charles we called the Clipper who wore a shirt with an eagle embroidered on the chest, and over the sand into the water. We swam out beyond the buoys, a long way out into the cool night water, riding the waves up and down and resting looking back at the lights of the houses huddled and clustered up the ridge and along the whole mile-long length of the beach until I began to come together again, I began to be Urlich Ambrose Skidmore in more than name, and to say over to myself those lines I would say at Nathan's restaurant, running them through my head like beads, then saying them aloud to the distant beach, no longer disintegrated but feeling in place of disintegration the beginnings of that huge unfocused feeling – yes it was there again: God, Fame, Nirvana, Great Love, Extinction – these were my desires, Aorewa, and you were swallowed up in them who wanted success for me, and happiness for us, and for yourself – what? Did I ever enquire?

'The house is empty,' Nathan Stockman said, walking from the kitchen into the big room still cluttered with restaurant chairs and tables. He felt he wanted to tidy the place. Not knowing where to start he took his violin out of its case and played a Bach partita in the dark directing it at the stars which he could see through the clerestory windows. Though he had carried his violin about with him since Felice had gone this was the first time he had taken it out and played it.

'Maybe she won't come back,' he said to himself, and for the first time he took that possibility calmly. But then he thought of Tony, 'Antoine', as he called himself professionally, and Nathan stopped playing Bach. He would kill Tony. If necessary he would kill them both. He would find out where they were . . .

He was pacing about the room now making cacophanous swoops across the strings with his bow. 'Kill,' his violin was saying. 'Kerjoink, *kill*!' She was a faithful servant, his instrument, she wanted what he wanted. He laid her gently back in her case and went to the kitchen, turning on the light and searching through the mess. He found an egg in the refrigerator and another on the sink slightly cracked and leaking among stalks of celery, but still fresh. He took out the pan to make himself an omelette and all at once he was very hungry. That was a good sign – and to celebrate it he turned on the radio.

'. . . knowing that you want what I want,' said the radio, 'a future free from intimidation and industrial anarchy and sabotage, free from fear . . .'

And you my little olive-skinned lover stepping up the beach from the water naked in the night, who can say except by guesswork and candlelight after the lapse of these thirty and more largely barren years what was in your mind? Were you Aorewa at that moment or were you de Thierry? I guess de Thierry because I remember the slow measured way you walked up the steps under the tamarisks holding yourself very straight while I held the gate for you and that as you crossed the lawn you were running your hands slowly, appreciatively over your breasts and that as soon as we went indoors you went to the mirror and turned yourself this way and that watching the light catch on the drops of water as they ran down from your hair and over the smooth hills and valleys of your body (*mon paysage*, I called you, when you were in a mood to be French) and gathered glistening in the bush that stood out black under your tight belly. I was rubbing myself hard with a towel, warming myself and exciting some substance back into my cold cock, but I suspected you were becoming ethereal again, that after that swim you would be rapt out of your body to a realm where I with my growing incumbrance would be inadmissible so it was not to you Curl Skidmore turned, Patagonia, but to the little kitchen (one appetite doing service for another) where he began to make toasted cheese and coffee, turning on the radio to listen while he worked.

' . . . should add that I was not misquoted,' said the radio, 'when I was reported upon my arrival back in New Zealand as having said there is no country in the world can hold a candle to this lovely land of ours. It's because I want to keep it that way that I call on you to support what I and my Government have done.'

And through the wall Mrs Battle sunk in her armchair with a book from the library and a box of chocolates and listening to the same station said to her forty-year-old son whose shirt displayed the emblem of the eagle, 'Turn it up Charles, it's Mr Holland.'

' . . . taken control of our waterfront industry,' said the radio, 'an industry vital to the health of our economy. I don't idly . . .'

And in his single room in the back yard of Mrs Hinchinghorn's Ponsonby boarding house little Kenny lay on his bed smoking and feeling depressed because Melior's letter was right, he couldn't take risks. While the crisis lasted he would just have to stay safely at home at night, read the paper, listen to the radio – and at that he rolled over and switched it on.

34

' . . . and their fellow-travellers would laugh,' said the radio, 'if I let these words appear to be empty of meaning and purpose . . .'

And Melior Farbro, rolling himself a cigarette and looking at Cecelia Skyways across the empty plates on the counter between them said, 'Let's listen to the PM's broadcast before we do the dishes.' And he limped over to the radio and turned it on.

' . . . an enemy within,' said the radio, 'just as unscrupulous, poisonous, treacherous and unyielding as the enemy without, an enemy who works by day and by night, who gnaws his way into the vitals of our economy as the codlin moth does to the apple . . .'

And Felice Stockman in a comfortable chair in the hotel room Tony had booked for them on Waiheke Island in the Hauraki Gulf, sat listening to the radio and watching the moon rise over the water, not trying this time to conceal the tears which at intervals for three days now had kept flooding her eyes, wondering (but not caring very much) who it was Tony had gone downstairs to phone.

' . . . why we have for the moment,' said the radio, 'limited the freedom of assembly and curtailed the right of any person, whoever he may be, to publish lies and promote disorder. My friends, let me assure you: We could give in to the strikers, but we won't. We could let tyranny replace democratic government . . .'

And at sea, hammering north through a light swell up the east coast of the northern cape of New Zealand's North Island, Jim and June who had gone to the radio room to send a telegram to their friends ashore were stopped from talking by the operator who said, 'Hold it a mo. Just let's listen to the rest of this and then we'll take your message.'

' . . . but we won't,' crackled the radio. 'We could let down every other worker who abides by the law – but we won't. I call on you . . .'

The omelette was fluffing up in the pan, the Prime Minister was puffing himself up into his peroration, when the phone rang. Nathan dropped the slice (it flipped a piece of half-cooked egg into the air) and darted this way and that knocking over a chair on his way to answer it. He recognized Tony's voice – that deep, resonant and deeply insincere tone. How could she have fallen for it? He was still panting from his dash to the phone and at the same time he knew he must hold his feelings in, pretend to be reasonable, accommodating, until he'd found out where they were hiding.

Tony didn't waste words. He offered a bargain. He would return Felice (he spoke of her as an object, a possession) but in exchange he thought Nathan should let him keep the MG.

Would she come back, Nathan asked.

Yes, Tony said she would if he told her to. Otherwise she would stay with him. They would go away together and Nathan wouldn't see her again.

'We must talk about it,' Nathan said, managing to keep the anger out of his voice. 'Can't you come here and we'll work out a bargain. Can you come tonight? In the morning?'

Tony was cool. He would come in the morning. But he was serious, he said, about the MG. It wasn't unreasonable, he said. He would be sorry to give up Felice and if he was giving her up he didn't see why he shouldn't get something in exchange. And no tricks. He wanted the registration papers and a receipt for £500 which of course wouldn't be paid – Felice would be the currency – the receipt signed by Nathan and saying, 'Being full payment for MG registration number etc.'

'I'll come in the morning,' Tony said. 'Have it all ready and I'll tell you where you can find her.'

Back in the kitchen Nathan found the omelette dried out and burned at the edges. He scraped it out into the rubbish and ran water into the pan. He didn't want to eat now. He walked about the house. She was coming back. He would beat her. He would

36

kill Tony. He must be calm. Nathan walked out on to the verandah and down on to the lawn.

The moon was coming up and there was light from the street lamp beyond the fence. He walked around and across the lawn thinking it out, touching the bark of one tree, then another. He opened the implement shed under the verandah and selected a slasher, an axe, a tomahawk, a mattock and a pick-handle. They lay on the grass and he began to place them around the garden – the axe in a fork of the biggest pohutukawa, the mattock in a rosemary bush, the pick-handle under the lemon-scented verbena, the tomahawk among branches of a lemon tree, and last the slasher which he slid into the mass of hydrangeas that grew by the gate and were half-hidden by it when it opened. He returned to the middle of the lawn, checking how the weapons were placed, the spacing between them. He went to the slasher and made sure it came free easily from its hiding place.

'There'll be a lot of blood,' he said.

Indoors the phone was ringing again. He made a dash for it. It was Tony again. He wanted to be sure that Nathan meant business. Nathan was to leave the papers and the receipt at Farbro's place. Tony would collect them there and if everything was in order he would then come and tell Nathan where he could find Felice.

'But how do I know you'll keep your part of the bargain?' Nathan asked.

'I'll keep it,' Tony said. 'You'll just have to take my word for that.'

Dear Prime Minister (wrote Cecelia Skyways) this isle is full of noises sounds and sweet airs that give delight and hurt not and I was very pleased to hear your voice on the air this evening, so reassuring and friendly and consoling and protecting especially to those of us who (as you said) want what you want. The thought of those other people who don't want what you want makes my electrified head go round and round. How can they be like that and isn't it always the way that just a handful spoil it for the others as they used to say at school and at Training College and in the convent (as I call it when I talk to Melior)? I hope you will go on damming the streams and making more and more electricity because there's nothing quite like an electrified head to straighten out a malcontent, I'm sure you know what I mean. As a matter of fact when your voice came on the wireless this evening I was pouring my friend Melior a cup of tea and I got such a surprise I forgot to stop, I just went on pouring, and Melior's cup overflowed on the table. In Christianity (here comes my convent training) that's supposed to mean plentitude – 'My cup runneth over' – the blessings of the Lord and all that, and I'm sure that's how you mean we should feel about you, a sort of father to your people in these troubled times. 'Yea though I walk through the valley of the shadow of death I shall fear no evil for Thou art with me' – and so on. I remember when I was a child I thought of the mess on the table and I used to wonder if he – that's He of course – minded. 'Thou preparest a table in the presence of mine enemies, Thou anointest my head with oil, my cup runneth over.' It all seemed to me very very messy. But you might know there's a Zen story (my Master in the Web told me this one) that uses the symbol of the overflowing cup quite differently. Someone goes to a famous Zen monk wanting instruction and the monk treats him to the tea ceremony and when it comes time to pour the monk keeps pouring until the cup overflows. So the visitor says, 'Excuse me, Master, but it's overflowing,' whereupon the monk clouts him with a stick and says, 'That cup is like your head. How can I put anything into it until you empty it of all you brought with you when you came.' A bit obvious? I suppose you're right, Prime Minister, he was very didactic that monk, but as you demonstrated so beautifully this evening there are times when it's important to get things straight. I'm typing this in the hut behind Melior's studio and I use a kerosene lantern because the hut doesn't have electricity. I should mention because it will interest you that when I came out here after doing the dishes with Melior I told my Master in the Web I had been listening to you on the wireless and he went into one of those fast gyrations which usually occur only if you reach up and touch him. He's what people call a daddy-longlegs – you know how they gyrate at a touch? – and I thought it was typical (and typically Zen-ish) of him to give me that sign and leave me to puzzle it out. It's my koan for the night: 'Why at the name of the Leader does the Master gyrate?' Answer: 'Already the moon has filled the empty cup.' Prime Minister I have to be frank with you. You promised me security, an end to fear, but you didn't mention the shadows out there in Melior's garden. Not one of them is a watersider, not even (you won't believe this) a communist, but they move as the wind stirs the leaves and though it may be true that their whispers are as gentle as the tongues of angels it is not true that I fear no evil. If I should rush out there and beat the shadows with a stick would my fear vanish? When you have beaten the wharfies with sticks what will have happened to yours? Prime Minister, my Master says (it must be our day for didactics) we must both empty the cup. Do come and have tea with me next time you find yourself at a loose end in Auckland. Yours sincerely, Cecelia Skyways.

And the moon that filled the cup, rising higher, shone on the sea, and on the tamarisks above the sea, and on the verandah above the tamarisks where Mrs Battle's forty-year-old son, Clipper Charles, still wearing his shirt with the embroidered eagle and still in a state of high excitement wrought in him by the Prime Minister's wireless promise to stand up to the wreckers, marched up and down the weather-worn tongue-in-groove flooring hitting a large saucepan with his mother's mixing spoon.

It shone on the silver head of Mrs Battle who had shuffled (step, drag) around the side of the house calling, 'Gurr-l, Gurr-l,' and who was now delivering from the courtyard up to the open sash window her triumphant monologue on the subject of the Prime Minister's speech.

It shone on the black shiny head of Patagonia de Thierry Aorewa Bennett known to Mrs Battle (though she preferred not to know her) as Pat who was incoherently and monosyllabically replying to the triumphant monologue, Curl having switched off all lights at the first sound of his landlady's (step, drag) call and refused to put forth his head.

And the moon that filled the cup did not shine on Urlich

Ambrose Skidmore who in the dark behind the curtains through which Patagonia's dark shiny incoherent and possibly giggling head protruded had removed her pants and with a certain caressing persuasion and a good deal of difficult angling this way and that was just succeeding in getting in from behind while she tried to talk to Mrs Battle.

And it was the same moon that sat in the arm of the pohutukawas and shone down into Nathan Stockman's now tranquil garden, picking out and dully shining upon a blade here, an axehead there, a heavy handle in a third place, while Nathan indoors sat at his desk getting the registration papers together and making out the receipt.

The last bus stopped at the top of the road and then roared away and as usual there was silence, no sound of footsteps out on the road, and then as happened sometimes there were footsteps and Melior, straining to listen, began the argument with himself, that those could not be little Kenny's footsteps, they were too slow, and too heavy, but on the other hand they might be, but hang on a second, surely the timing wasn't right, if the owner of the steps had got off that bus he wouldn't have got along the road so soon, not at that pace, so it couldn't be anyone off the bus, but on the other hand it might be . . .

And then the footsteps turned in at the gate and came down the path through the garden and around the side of the studio and Melior wanting to leap from his chair found he couldn't and sat quite still, calling in a slightly wobbly voice, 'Come in,' when there was a knock. So the door opened and the footsteps came tentatively forward and there in the half light was not Kenny but Nathan Stockman looking as though he'd been dragged backward through the hedge, and holding out to Melior while mumbling something about Felice and the MG and the cook, two or three papers and documents, and with an expression on his face that mixed excitement and apprehension so confusingly Melior laughed, forgetting his disappointment for a moment and said, 'Nathan, my boy, you look like a candidate for the ovens.'

* * *

Or let's approach it like any conventional tale and say, Once there was a violinist called Nathan Stockman whose wife ran away with the cook and who planned to kill the cook to get his revenge. So he waited in his suburban garden where he had planted weapons, skulking among hydrangeas behind the gate in the board fence while the sun rose higher and the day grew hotter and the suburb stirred and woke and got moving and as the hours passed Nathan wondered and began to doubt and to worry but at last the phone rang – three rings and then silence, three rings again and silence. That was Melior. That was the signal. Melior had handed over the papers and the receipt and that should mean Tony was on his way – and very soon there was the sound of the MG pulling up outside. Engine idling, engine switched off, silence. Car door opens and shuts, footsteps slowly cross gravelled path to gate. Gate unlatching, opening, obscuring Nathan's view as footsteps advance tentatively into garden. Nathan kicks door shut, lifts slasher and brings it down with such violence he has to collapse backward among hydrangeas to prevent it falling where it's aimed and splitting Felice's head in two. Recovers, dragging himself up from among hydrangeas hearing MG start up outside. Pushes Felice aside (she falls heavily over her suitcase, letting out sopranoshriek) drags at gate, rushes through still carrying slasher, and across pavement as car accelerates away. Yell of rage from Nathan swinging slasher overhead and letting go. Smashes through back windscreen of MG and buries itself in back of driver's seat. MG stalls a moment, veers across street, straightens and pulls away, vanishing into traffic up on Hurstmere Road.

And the same morning is delivered to Curl and Pat a telegram transmitted the previous night from a liner travelling north-ward, east of North Cape, by an operator still preoccupied (as were its senders) by the Prime Minister's broadcast picked up at sea: LATER MIGHT NOT BE SOON ENOUGH THINK YOU SHOULD FOLLOW AT ONCE LOVE JIM & JUNE.

THREE

An Ordinary Saturday in Summer

And now the shadow cast by the cabbage tree at the centre of the white courtyard with the green border must be longer at noon but nobody measures it because it is the late summer that always settles into the hottest and driest weather. Today it is Saturday, well past the meridian, and the sand is littered with inert bodies and the water is agitated with active bodies and in the verandah flat one end of which overlooks the beach there is another kind of agitation, an agitation of the spirit and of the hands and of the two voices that have gone up a register even in the hoarse whispers they are maintaining back and forth, exchanging the fact that *they* are coming, they have been seen on the drive, they are crossing the courtyard, they are approaching the door, they are knocking at the door, they are calling, 'It's us,' and, 'Can ve come in?' and, 'Ooh-hoo Early, it's your mother dear,' while the hoarse whispers fly from Curl to Pat and from Pat to Curl as they hurtle this way and that knocking into one another in the narrow space making the final adjustments, the last tidyings, and checking especially that his sleeping bag and pillow are conspicuous on the divan bed in some vain hope that the momma at least if not the father might believe that though they do quite unacceptably and against all odds and in the teeth of family protests share a flat it is on a basis which is 'Platonic', and not Melior Farbro's Platonic but the Platonism of the popular mind, meaning 'Look no hands' and no anything else either. 'We are just good friends, Momma.' And, 'Don't be so suspicious.' And, 'It's just a way of economizing.' And, 'We find we can study better together.'

And, 'Don't be so old-fashioned.' And, 'Everything isn't what it seems' (it isn't of course – it's worse). But now the door is opening a fraction and a fraction more and there is looking in a large smiling face under a white hat with a brim so broad Pat is thinking if she sits dead centre it will maybe fit between the windows on one side and the mat-covered wall on the other with only a little bending at the outer edges; and Curl is registering that she – his momma – is inn ein goot mood, happy and smiling and engulfing, which sends at once and willy-nilly and against all his best efforts to the contrary a heavy tram-track down between his eyebrows to darken that pale smooth plane of forehead behind which the novels of the future are secretly winding. The door is opened wide, then wider to admit them but it looks to Curl and to Pat as if it could never open wide enough, they are so huge, the Momma almost as tall as her son and twice the girth, the father towering over her and carrying under his waistcoat and inside the tailored expanse of his trouser-top a round mountain over which is draped his gold watch chain from which in turn hangs the medallion that shows he is a Member of Parliament and allows him free passage on the railways. Curl is embraced first, long and hard, the silent duration of the embrace signalling (he knows the signals and she knows he knows them) the emotion she is suppressing, the suffering she has gone through but which she is not (brave little woman-mountain) going to inflict on the company today – and while he submits to this hot engulfment, awkwardly clamped under one big arm and foolishly fondled by the other, he catches a glimpse across the yard of Mrs Battle unlocking Jim and June's flat and standing back to let a hangdog pair, whom he nonetheless recognizes as Nathan and Felice Stockman, step inside to look. But now Pat is being embraced too, the Momma is embarking on a new policy, it not having been possible in the past to embrace something which she did not recognize existed, calling her Dear and My dear and Patty-dear and Patricia (she doesn't believe anyone was ever called Patagonia – that is just one of Curl's stories) and handing her a square tin painted with butterflies in which there is a beautiful iced cake ('I know how my Curl luffs his cake – he hass been missing ze Momma's cooking haven't you sveet?') and two pots of jam while the father detaches one of the two large kits he carries revealing that it is full of carrots potatoes beans tree-tomatoes chokos peaches plums and some early apples. So there is now the problem of seating involving an elaborate side-stepping and turning motion, a reversing of engines and a certain amount of straining against the wharf piles and bollards, until the two visiting bottoms have been manoeuvred by the tugs which are at home in this narrow harbour into a single berth – the divan bed under the matting-covered wall (Pat's cubist piece is down for the day), there to recline among cushions, while Curl and Pat, who cannot sit exactly opposite without creating an embarrassing knee-to-knee crush between visitors and visited, angle themselves a little up-stream and down-stream respectively (and respectfully) pointing inward toward the parental pair. The Momma, it should be said, has been persuaded in this exercise to remove her hat which has been transported together with the father's jacket and hat (he now sits starkly informal in waistcoat and tie, the springy silver bands which hold his sleeves back from his wrists glinting over his biceps) to the bedroom which is supposed to be (and often is) Pat's alone. The talk is first of money and of how they are managing to pay the two pounds five shillings per week charged by Mrs Battle and Curl tells them his work in the foundry every weekend (he doesn't admit to giving up lectures to work there full-time) is enough together with the allowance Pat gets from her family (he doesn't mention the allowance has been stopped since she left the hostel). The father says there will soon be part-time work available on the wharves and Curl says he won't take work on the wharves if the Government sets up a scab union there and the father says Sid Holland is coming on strong but there's not much parliamentary Labour can do about it because the union bosses on the wharf bought this lot, and Curl says the Opposition is sitting on the fence as usual, and the Momma who never runs away from a fight on her own behalf but is distressed if others, especially those she calls her 'menfolk', go into battle, says that it is a lovely glittering day, that the yachts are beautiful on the Gulf, that it's strange how dark Rangitoto looks even under the brightest sun, that they are lucky young people to have found such a nice flat but she hopes it doesn't stop them getting on with their studies, that the walls look flimsy and soon the cold weather will be here, that Curl needs vitamin C as well as cakes he is so prone to colds, and that she and the father have brought their bathing suits and would like to 'haf a svim before ze uftanoon tea'.

An ordinary Saturday in summer when Mr and Mrs Skidmore are visiting their boy who is living certainly in Takapuna and possibly in sin in Mrs Battle's verandah flat with brown Pat Bennett, and Nathan and Felice Stockman are looking at Mrs Battle's outhouse flat wondering whether they should move in there until they decide where to go next, and Mrs Battle is step-dragging back to her kitchen leaving them to consider, and Charles Battle is sitting in the half-dark of the fowl-house smelling the dusty straw of the nests and thinking. Down in Devonport Rex Fairburn is pouring Ron Mason a beer out in the garden and saying the dry weather will bugger his lettuces and cursing the printer Bob Lowry who has taken the young poet Baxter (who is supposed to be reading with them this evening) visiting the wineries of the Henderson Valley. And across the harbour in his room at the back of Mrs Hinching-horn's Ponsonby boarding house Ken Blayburn is lying on his bed with a notebook and pencil and Best Bets and Raceform and with the radio going beside his bed, playing his favourite solo game and putting imaginary bets on the horses and keeping count of winnings and losses. (So far today he is up £312/5/6.) An ordinary Saturday in summer Melior Farbro thinks hoeing his garden, but why do we kid ourselves? It would be just as ordinary if it was pissing down and the leaves in the garden were hanging heavy with warm rain and the air inside was so moist you felt as if you were living in a tank. 'On thee, on thee the unswerving season smiles' – Kipling on Auckland (Thank you, Mr K!), and today you might think he was right, but there were the other days when you might think 'On thee, on thee the un-smiling season swerves' was nearer to the mark. Not the best cli-mate for human growth or human thought, Melior concludes, but a great climate for gardens, and he pushes his hoe into the volcanic soil and tries to keep his mind off the new series that is going its own way day by day and giving him a mixture of excitement and anxiety. An ordinary day in summer for Melior's two cats, Agatha and Christie, elegantly draped over the back step, but now they rise together into a pair of furred arches, hissandspit, and around the corner of the house along the path into the back garden comes the neighbour's dog, Rosh, who ignores them, lifts his leg to squirt a nasty orange-coloured urine at a big cabbage, scratches a few token times on either side, and walks with springy confidence up to Melior who pats his head and scratches his back with the hoe while the dog lifts his chin and twists his head and the skin creeps visibly on his back. Through the half-open door of the hut Melior can see Cecelia Skyways sitting cross-legged on the floor in silent meditation, her skirt drawn up to make room for the posture (lotus? Melior wonders) exposing her round white nun-knees which he thinks ought to be calloused from kneeling at prayer but appear not to be. The inside of the hut is changing, becoming spare and plain, with island matting on the floor got for her off the banana boats by young Skidmore, and there is a poem in red and black ink on white parchment hanging from the ceiling. Her typewriter goes flat-stick in the mornings and what she shows him is a kind of prose-poetry, beautiful and skittish and brilliant and free-flowing, and she's not troubled (as Melior is troubled when he thinks of his new paintings) about what people will think of it. She just does it, she's free, she has no public.

'You'll bugger your hips, Cecil,' he calls to her. Her eyes flicker but she keeps on staring at the wall.

'Osteo-arthritis,' he says, and this time she gives up.

'You've spoiled my medit,' she says, but really it hasn't been going well, she has begun to think about the next of her Random Letters to Unknown Quantities which she intends to write to Her Majesty Queen Salote of Tonga.

Rosh is springing away down the path again. Agatha and Christie have come down out of their self-made arches. Melior leans the hoe against the wall and limps indoors to put on the kettle. There, just inside, is the parcel of illegal leaflets, delivered yesterday off a battered old truck by a man called Fred, and on the counter between the kitchen and the studio the precious note that came with them:

Dear Mel,
Can you see these get handed out at your poetry reading? Ron Mason told me about it, and we have to use every outlet we can get. I can tell you, things are bad.
                    Yours ever,
                    Ken.

'Yours ever,' Melior repeats, filling the jug. 'Yours occasionally' would be more like it. And these days it might as well be 'Yours never'. But still the sight of the note puts him in a good humour. He's glad there's something Ken wants him to do.

Nathan sits in an old armchair, staring out beyond the tamarisks towards Rangitoto, while Felice runs her finger along the window sill, testing it for dust. Mrs Battle has step-dragged back across the courtyard leaving them to consider the little flat and let her know whether they want it at thirty-seven and six a week. Felice sighs. The days are full of her sighing and her tears. She is ashamed, she is contrite, she says she won't do it again but he doesn't quite believe her and neither does she.

'It's a nice view,' he says wearily.

'But we had a better one,' she replies and he doesn't deny it.

'It's all my fault,' she says, and he doesn't contradict her. He's sorry the beautiful house must be sold but for him there is a grain of satisfaction in it. It's her punishment and he's glad to see her punished even though at the same time he wants to take her in his arms and console and forgive. The flat has only two rooms, a bed-sitting room looking out to the beach and a kitchen. A two-roomed outhouse covered with passion fruit vines contains the bathroom and laundry which they will share with Curl and Pat

'We won't be able to practise at the same time,' Felice says.

'One of us can use the bathroom,' he says, and as he says it there is pleasure for him in the recognition that whichever of them should have to practise in the bathroom it will cause her pain and guilt.

'We'll take turns,' he says, and then he feels shot through with compassion as he sees the tears spring into her eyes.

'I'll never sing again,' she says, but he can't let that pass either.

'So you kept me from the Wellington job for nothing,' he says.

Across the yard the door of the verandah flat has opened and two huge white figures in striped bathing suits come down the steps, the man-mountain first, stopping at the bottom step to take the hand of the woman-mountain who follows and who steps into the glaring white yard as if into a pool of light. Hand in hand they make their way through the trellis gate across the lawn to the front gate, down to the beach and over the sand into the water. The man-mountain strikes out boldly after a neat dive but the woman-mountain darts forward and back, surprisingly nimble and graceful in the shallows, before finding the courage to launch herself.

'There's no room for our things,' Felice says, sullen now.

'We'll sell them,' he says brutally. 'I'll tell Mrs Battle we'll move in next week. We'd better get back and make the house ready for the poetry reading.' But he doesn't move from his chair, and she sinks into one, and together they stare silently out to sea.

An ordinary Saturday in summer. Ken Blayburn is no longer lying on his bed at the back of Mrs Hinchinghorn's Ponsonby boarding house. He has just dropped an imaginary £200 on the fifth at Ellerslie and decided to call it a day. Even as topweight Regal Fox should have outstayed them but she got checked at the turn and wasn't in contention over the final furlong.

'Bugger it, I'm going out.' And Ken is combing down his hair with a little Brylcream and adjusting his hat.

An ordinary Saturday in summer and Charles Battle is still breathing the scent of dusty straw, and thinking. The hens come in ones and twos through their little square hole in the wall of the fowl-house to look at him and go away. Out at Oratia in the Henderson Valley the young Baxter from the south has gone around the side of the wine-shed for a leak against the corrugated iron. 'Where the fuck am I,' he wonders, staring up at the hills covered in tree-ferns. Down in Devonport Rex Fairburn is cracking another bottle of DB, and here in Takapuna Melior Farbro is limping more heavily than usual, thrown off balance by the weight of the parcel in his rucksack, and impeded by Rosh who hasn't yet settled down and is still leaping up at him with pleasure at being invited to come for a walk. But Farbro doesn't mind the dog, nor the weight of the parcel in his rucksack, nor the heat which strikes up off the pavement bringing the sweat out on his brow. Before leaving he has allowed himself to look again at this morning's painting and again in spite of anything that reason and past experience might say to the contrary he's shot through with a feeling of confidence that this series is new and exciting and the best thing he has ever done. This morning the human figures were very small, little black dwarfs against the light and the sky very pale, and then into that sky before he thought about it went one of those circles but this wasn't a speech balloon it was a cloud that was going to bring rain, not a cloud like any cloud you see in the sky but a paintingcloud, and then again there was that rushing forward impulse which he'd decided always to give in to as long as it continued and in a few strokes he painted in black letters that matched the black human figures under the cloud and looked almost like a repetition of them the word CLOUD with a small arrow pointing at the cloud.

Melior stops abruptly in the street, almost trips, because Rosh in full bouncy stride has suddenly thrown himself down on the pavement, one back leg pointing stiffly skywards, and is going snuff-snuff-snuff snap-snap-snap after a flea somewhere in the region of his balls.

'I suppose you know what you're doing, boy,' Melior says, 'but it looks bloody dangerous to me.'

The tin with the butterflies painted on its lid is open on the yellow table in front of the three-speed tablegram and beside the lamp that has a Japanese design on its shade, and inside the tin there is what is left of the cake. It is white and pink with chocolate facings, its architecture classical, Corinthian perhaps, or Doric, now in ruins, and the Momma who designed and built it and who has had much to do with its demolition is herself pink and white but without the facings. She is pressing a third slice on the father who is worrying silently about the size of his stomach but reasoning that the swim has justified a little more intake than usual, while son Urlich is proving the Momma's point about his love of and need for her cake.

'He luffs his Momma's cake more zan he luffs his Momma,' she says, looking for the denial which he, however, fails to offer, while Pat (the Momma thinks of her as Patricia) is sunk in a chocolate silence impenetrable to the European eye and consequently sinister and threatening. But creeping up behind them, so to speak, is the welling, whelming, soon to be engulfing Wagnermusic of the record (one of the new long-players) the Momma has asked Curl to put on the tablegram which she bought him for his twenty-first birthday. It stirs somewhere below the cake and spreads upward into the back of the neck and up through the scalp branching outward as well into the shoulders and down the arms. It is still quiet, only beginning, it has not silenced the talk, but Curl feels it working there and knows the Momma feels it too and that it will soon extend outward to gather in the father and the Pat, locked in her chocolate silence, and that it will reach out to cast a twilight of the gods over the courtyard and the cabbage tree. But before this has happened there is a tap at the door, it is Melior, his green rucksack, that is usually full of vegetables when he calls, so heavy on his shoulder Curl thinks it must contain a pumpkin, but at once Melior begins to withdraw saying, 'You have visitors,' and that he will just drop his bundle of pamphlets which are for distribution at the reading tonight and then he'll be off. But Curl tells him he must stay and the Momma offers him tea, and Patagonia has faintly smiled in the instant before she turned finally to stone; but it is perhaps none of these appeals so much as a single long chord of the Wagnermusic that throws a web over him and persuades him to stay, collapses him in fact, so that his knees sag and he sinks down on the concrete step murmuring that they mustn't try to rearrange the seating, he will just take his tea on the step. It is the Momma who has turned Pat to stone and the Momma triumphant now (she has heard of this Melior Farbro, oh yes!) who pours the tea and cuts the cake and hands them to him amid the gathering storm of the Wagnermusic and at the same moment, as if drawn out by it from the cave of their present hopelessness, Nathan and Felice emerge from Jim and June's flat and seem to cross the yard on wheels or on wires, their feet not touching the ground, and it is you, dear terrible Momma, who hands them down the canvas chairs which they place in the courtyard at the bottom of the steps, and the cups and the cake which they balance on their knees. I write it all as if it is happening now because that is how it seems, terrible Momma, and I address you these almost thirty years on, look for you to listen wherever you are, under the ground or out in space, with the father and with Melior and with the legions of the dead, knowing you will remember the yard that day when we all stepped outside the boundaries of time, gathered into the heavens by the ride of the Valkyrie, so that I recognize you and the father in your eternal forms, two white clouds edged with pink, huge and travelling hardly at all out across the Gulf beyond the island called Rangitoto which means bloody sky. Because the Wagnermusic had taken hold of us, Melior had begun to conduct, and you had sung yourself silently then audibly into the role of Brunnhilde before the fabulous Felice could open her soprano throat (she had some cake to dispose of first). But now the Felicevoice was going up and coming down out of the air around the cabbage tree in the role of a Valkyrie (Grimgerde, perhaps) with that strange mountain cry 'Hoiatoho! Hoiatoho! Heyaha! Heyaha!' and I was swinging in with some of the bass notes of Wotan's anger while Nathan played an imaginary fiddle spilling his tea and breaking his cup on the concrete (we left it there while the music lasted) and even the father who couldn't sing a note in tune was beating a sort of no-time on his bemedalled belly while Patagonia's impenetrable impenitent stone face was the noble stillness at the heart of the storm. So it cast a spell over us and even when it was over and they were getting ready to depart and it was explained that Melior was leaving illegal pamphlets still the father didn't as he would normally have done complain that Curl was taking risks, playing a dangerous game, that the son of an MP had a responsibility not to cause his father public embarrassment, and the son didn't reply (as he would have done) that the father lacked courage and that if Labour was going to lose an election because of the wharf dispute they might as well lose with a clear conscience. It was one family row, a rare one, that exists only in that parallel dimension where things which might have happened are kept as in an archive of unpublished writing or a library of never-projected film, and we seemed to separate happy, smiling, full of love, and knowledge, and perhaps even regret, at least with a sense of mortality, which was as well, and with a lot of cake under the belt, went our different ways towards divorce, defeat and death.

Are you there Early?

That's Pat. It's you isn't it? Pat?

Aorewa. I think I stopped being Pat a quarter of a century ago.

Aorewa. Correction noted. Welcome. You can call me Urlich.

Urlich. OK Early, got it. But look – I have one or two objections. Do you mind?

Objections? But you told me it was all going on inside my head.

You'd prefer I went.

No don't go. Pat? Aorewa? Are you there? Fuck it why don't you use a telephone?

You don't sound very professorial, Ambrosia.

This is the leather-topped desk under the clerestory light with the white stuccoed wall and the de Thierry and the two Farbros. I don't get paid for being professorial here. So now – you have some objections.

Only if you're interested.

I'm interested.

I mean in getting at the truth. The facts.

The truth. The facts. They're not quite the same sweetheart. But fire away. I'm listening.

You're not taking me seriously Oilrich.

All ears. Pencil's at the ready.

I know that tone.

Ao please.

Well to start with 'Sunk in a chocolate silence' . . .

OK so you weren't chocolate.

Not even milk chocolate Early.

True. But I've said somewhere else you were olive-skinned.

So what are your readers going to think? One minute I'm olive, the next I'm chocolate.

It was something to do with the cake wasn't it? I think that's what put it in my head. The momma was pink and white like the icing and the Ao was chocolate like the facings.

That's a hell of a way to write history!

You keep telling me it's my book . . .

And what about the momma. She was small.

She seemed pretty big to me.

She was small Early. She was fat but she was small. And why have you given her that Katzenjammer accent?

It's how I hear her in my head.

She didn't talk like that.

So the momma in my head has a Katzenjammer accent, the momma in yours hasn't. It's what I mean about the facts and the truth. They're not always the same.

You're supposed to be a professor Curlyboy. Facts are facts aren't they? The truth is the truth.

Ao do you remember the seawall picture? It's here – just along from the Farbros. What would you say if I told you my head seen from behind was never a triangle?

Patagonia?

OK Early. Point taken. Don't go on about it. But look, just one small point. I mean a question.

It's nine thirty. But go ahead. I have a minute or two.

What became of Rosh?

So there is or there ought to be the question of what became of

Rosh who had been accompanying Melior Farbro on his walk through Takapuna carrying the pamphlets, but who didn't appear during the musical scene in the yard. Rosh had run on ahead of Melior down the drive and had met Mrs Battle who struck at him with her broom at the same time shouting to Charles to come and help – the spaniel was trespassing again. Rosh retreated, found a gap in the hedge, and made his way across the lawn next door pursued by small potatoes which Clipper Charles, emerging from his fowl-house think, threw at his tail. So Rosh missed the Wagnermusic which his sensitive nature might not have enjoyed (he used to howl when the girl next door played her oboe) and the cake which he would have liked a lot. Down on the sand some boys threw a stick for him and he chased it into the water. What happened after that isn't recorded, but by six o'clock that evening he was curled up as usual with his old mother in front of the wireless set hearing (or not hearing) news from London of the tonnage of bombs dropped in North Korea, the movement of Chinese troops there, and the fact that UN forces were once again retreating from the ruins of Seoul.

An ordinary Saturday in summer, evening now after the Wagnermusic in the concrete yard, the sun gone from the windows of Nathan Stockman's house, the excitement of a poetry reading banned, or almost banned, under the Emergency Regulations, the local poets Fairburn and Mason to be joined by the young marvel Baxter from the south, the beautiful broad room recently a restaurant already full, the windows pushed out wide and those who couldn't get inside sitting or standing on the decking at one side and on the verandah at the other, a cluster of people still at the door unable to find a place from which to see and hear . . .

Melior had arrived early with Cecelia Skyways and they found two seats well placed but near enough to the door for Cecelia not to feel trapped. But before the reading began she vanished. Melior had been staring up through the clerestory glass at the high dark branches of the pohutukawas lit by lights from the house and when he turned again to speak to Cecelia she was gone. He stood up and looked for her but there was no sign. Down the room near the low stage set up with a rostrum and a light Melior could see the young Skidmore, very pale and tense, and beside him his brooding Patagonia, olive-skinned and inscrutable. And at the same time from the other end of the room came a stirring, a shuffling movement to left and right as the audience made space for the poets who made their way slowly towards the stage moving strangely abreast. Rex Fairburn, tall and with a Wordsworthian nose, wore his usual khakis and sandals. Mason was more conventionally dressed (tweed jacket, white shirt and tie, flannel trousers and black shoes) but the clothes were shabby and ill-fitting. Between them, at first hidden, but then, as they advanced into the room, clearly visible, was the young Baxter who despite the heat wore a big raincoat with wide lapels over a black open-necked shirt. On his feet he wore goloshes over shoes, and looking down at them Melior saw that although Baxter's feet were making walking movements they weren't touching the ground. The two older men were carrying him by the elbows, and as he passed at close range Melior saw that the eyes in his long mournful face were barely open. There were only two steps up to the platform and Baxter seemed to put his feet to them. Half stumbling, half carried, he was piloted up to his chair into which he slumped, falling forward as his supports left him, so he finished hanging forward over his knees staring at his own feet.

Mason read first. He had a tin ear Melior thought, but they were good poems and when he read:

Garrisons pent up in a little fort
with foes who do but wait on every side
knowing the time soon comes when they shall ride
triumphant over those trapped and make sport
of them: when those within know very short
is their hour and no aid can betide:
such men as these not quarrel and divide
but friend and foe are friend in their hard sort

Melior found himself thinking of little Ken and thinking, in the stillness that came over the audience, that was what they'd

55

meant in the days when they used to talk about 'solidarity'. And when Mason followed it with his angry sonnet about the American General Douglas MacArthur who, looking down at dead North Korean soldiers, had said it was a good sight for his old eyes, the poem raised a cheer.

Fairburn followed Mason and you could count on him to entertain. He would play shamelessly to the gallery, Melior knew it, but he would make his audience happy.

And meanwhile Cecelia Skyways is along the beach. She has panicked and run away from the crowd and now she is walking along at the water's edge in the dark saying poems over to herself in a fine clear child-voice, delivering a reading of her own out to sea and up to the stars. She doesn't care that she has run away, she won't let herself care. Caring is not for those whose heads have been electrified. Caring is not for those who attend to the wisdom of Bodhidharma of the Web. Caring is not for the Lady of Shalott who may see the world in a mirror but not face to face. But Cecelia has wanted to hear the poets read – to hear Fairburn and Mason and the young marvel from the south. She has wanted to hear Curl Skidmore who is not part of the reading but is to be allowed five minutes to do his Takapuna piece before the second half. She wonders whether it might still be possible. Should she go back and look for a place on the verandah or on the decking? – but she doesn't turn, she continues on her way. The beach is empty, the dark shape of Rangitoto just visible across the Gulf. As she walks along she picks out Mrs Battle's house. She has never been there but Melior has pointed it out to her. She walks up the sand to look closer, climbs the concrete steps and goes through the gate under the tamarisks. From the lawn she can see into the front sitting-room where Mrs Battle sits at a table playing patience, Charles in an armchair nearby turning the dials of the wireless. Cecelia goes through the gate in the vine-covered trellis, into the darkness of the little white courtyard. She tries the door of Curl Skidmore's verandah flat and finds it unlocked. Inside she doesn't dare turn on the lights but her eyes grow accustomed to the dark. She is frightened of the shadows but she inflicts this

56

fear on herself. It's her punishment for running away. She stands looking out to sea from the beach end of the verandah and then feels her way along the length of it, through the little kitchen and into the bedroom. There she stands very still, trembling, but breathing the bedroom smells, the smells of cosmetics and of bodies. In the dim light she can see the shine of two large mirrors, angled this way and that towards the double bed. From under the pillows she takes his pyjamas and Pat's. She crushes them against her face, enjoying the softness of the material and breathing deeply through it. The sense of such human proximity makes her feel weak at the knees, and she subsides on to the bed, still holding the pyjamas to her face.

As the applause for Fairburn dies away there is an uneasy stirring, a sense of embarrassment. The young Baxter is still hanging forward over his knees, staring at his goloshes. But at a word from Rex Fairburn he can be seen in the shadow beyond the single light at the rostrum to stir, to shift himself. The room grows silent and the young Baxter's papers can be heard shuffling. He heaves himself out of his chair, lurches to the rostrum and puts down on it his manuscripts and books, hesitates for a moment, pushing back from his broad pale horizontally striated brow a lank lock, and then shuffles away into the shadow as if representing physically his own withdrawal into the dimmer recesses of the alcohol-soaked brain where his poems are nonetheless preserved fresh and dry. He is now only a shadow in the shadow at the edge of the light and from this shadow issues a round rich fruity voice which has also about it a grinding edge.

'Mey first poo-em . . .' he begins. Baxter is underway.

And as the voice of the young Baxter spins light out of shadow in the crowded room the finger-ends of Cecelia Skyways turn loneliness and failure into vision and ecstasy.

'Consider Takapuna . . .' So began the brilliant young Skidmore from along the beach. It was a beginning that could have been the beginning of a lifetime in which his 'Takapuna piece' would be endlessly repeated, ever more professionally, ever more satisfyingly, because in those minutes (he had promised five and took twelve before the interruption occurred) the young Skidmore – Curl – Urlich Ambrose – felt (and he was not wrong in feeling, but would believe he had been wrong) that he had held an audience on the merest inflexion of the voice, on the lift and fall of a verb, on the slightest accompanying movement of hand or tilt of head. Having felt himself drained, dragged down, clawed white, vampired by nervousness, having sweated and dry-mouthed his way unhearing through the first half, having failed to run away only because his limbs would not carry him, having stood at the rostrum when his moment arrived, silent because he could make no sound come, and then by some gift of the gods, some opening of the heavens, having dragged out of himself in just the full round not shouting yet into-every-corner-reaching voice it needed his opening 'Consider Takapuna', having so far managed himself and embarked upon his 'piece', there was no looking back. It was like the yacht that is dragged and heaved and hauled and lumbered down the beach over shells through shallows, dead weight all the way, and all at once finding its draught, canvas bellying to the wind, skims weightless away out into the Gulf towards Rangitoto and beyond – beyond, if you should wish, if you should be mad enough, through the gateway to the world. A lifetime it might have been, Curl Skidmore, a lifetime of your Takapuna piece, a solo virtuoso performance in every city town settlement and back-blocks nowhere, in every school assembly, community centre, RSA hall and Maori meeting house up and down the country. And who was it saved you from this travesty, this stage cardboard caricature of the literary life? It was not Melior Farbro, suppressing a yawn as he acknowledged to himself that although the piece was flimsy you were indeed winning your audience with it. It was not Ron Mason who quite liked the piece but thought it lacked ideological content. It was not Rex Fairburn, who, going over in his mind the jokes he had delivered 'off the cuff', and the ones he was saving for the second half, was too preoccupied to listen to you at all. It was not, of course, Jim Baxter, who had risen mightily to his task out of an alcoholic miasma and was now sunk back into it where he would remain until called in the second half to read again. It was not Cecelia Skyways, who as you began to read was tidying your bed, concealing all trace of her presence there, and as you ran on towards your tenth minute was making her way back along the sand with Nathan Stockman's house once again in sight. It was not even the olive-skinned Patagonia, who, though she had sat through your reading asking herself Why is he saying *that*? or observing inwardly *That* isn't true, didn't believe her own response was worth considering. Certainly it was not your audience as a whole who were, as you rightly suspected, and as you afterwards quite wrongly doubted, pliable in the palm of your expressive hand. You were saved, Curl Skidmore, by that redoubtable Sergeant Robinson, the same who on the night after the Queen Street riots in 1932 had sat squarely astride his horse at Hall's Corner, Takapuna, and turned aside a mob that without his opposition would undoubtedly have reduced the little shopping centre of those days to another Red Ruin. Two decades older but still redoubtable, backed up by other members of the force and by a hastily mustered local dozen of unofficial supporters, Sergeant Robinson, in receipt of a tip-off that a meeting in support of the strike (under the guise of a poetry reading) would be taking place at the house of the violinist Nathan Stockman down on the beach, had rallied his forces quietly in the lower grounds of the Mon Desir Hotel, and having received from his informant inside confirmation that illegal pamphlets had been handed out during the interval and that several references to the strike had already been made from the stage, set them in motion shortly after the second half began. So it was, Curl Skidmore, that twelve minutes into your five-minute slot you were interrupted by a voice less subtle but no less theatrical and penetrating than your own, calling, 'That's enough of that now,' and telling the audience to move out leaving all 'illegal liderachewer' behind. So it was that Cecelia Skyways, arriving on the decking outside just in time to see you, hand raised, voice extended and beautifully modulated, describing the movement of a gull over water, should next minute have been frightened back into the garden and down on to the sand by an eruption of violence from within, which grew as audience on the one hand and police and their supporters on the other confronted one another. Cecelia listened from the darkness as the shouting grew louder, the sound of heavy feet thudded on the floorboards, glass smashed, furniture broke, shouts screams sirens sounded, and last of all smoke, flames, the fire for which each side would blame the other (but only one story – the official one – would appear in print) billowed and roared through the roof. In the end there was nothing to be done but stand back and look while Nathan's and Felice's beautiful house, designed by brother Emil to be a piece of 'real architecture', flamed up under the overhanging arches of the pohukukawas. So no one told you, Curl Skidmore, that you had been a success, because no one remembered. It was all obliterated by the fight, the fire, the recriminations. Only you remembered what you had read and how your audience had seemed to react, and hearing not a word from anyone about your performance you decided you had been mistaken, that you must scrap your 'Takapuna piece' and go back, at least to contemplating, if not actually to writing, the two novels still waiting wound up and tucked away there on the scrolls inside your head.

FOUR

Marking Time

Mrs Hinchinghorn's boarding house, well known as it is to readers of our peninsular literature, has been described only in its latterday appearance after the siting of a raincoat factory next door (a Maori sandblasted on the glass door, it will be remembered, carried a feather cloak in one hand and a plastic mac in the other) had cramped its style and spoiled its proportions. That cramping took place in the sixties, and demolition followed a decade later. But in the first year of the second half of the twentieth century Mrs Hinchinghorn's house looked pretty much as it must have looked in the first year of the first half – somewhat seedier, in need of a fresh coat of white paint and the replacement here and there of a dry-rotted or borer-peppered plank in its weatherboard structure; but for all that, grand, like Mrs Hinchinghorn herself, product of a more spacious age. Its sash windows and verandahs at front and side were generous, as was the stud of its rooms. The yard at the back dropped into a gully through which in the early days a stream had flowed down into the harbour. That was at a time when this had been a respectable part of town. But now the gully was overgrown with fennel and stinkweed, the stream vanished into a rat-infested culvert, the concrete path to the clothes line was broken and the lawn on either side full of weeds and holes. In every way Mrs H's establishment was a mixed blessing, but to Ken Blayburn the pluses outweighed the minuses. It was here he had come to live after returning from the war, and it was the chance to move from the upstairs room Mrs Hinchinghorn had first allotted him to the room in the back yard which had confirmed him in residence. The outhouse room was only a few yards down the broken path, and Ken liked the quiet and isolation. Down the yard he could lie alone on his bed with his door open in the warm weather looking down into the green wilderness of the gully hearing the water echoing quietly through the culvert after a shower of rain, thinking his own thoughts. But now the strike had come (even the men, he noticed, had begun to call the lockout a strike) and Ken found himself lying and looking out for more hours of the day and night than could be enjoyed. A kind of inertia set in. Because there was little pressure on him to do anything he did almost nothing, spent longer and longer hours dozing and dreaming, and when there was work to be done for the union, he found it hard to rouse himself from his torpor.

And while Ken Blayburn lies dozing on his bed, the thin arms of Curl Skidmore, stiff at the elbows, and through the arms the shoulders and the neck and the head and the spine, are jolted tut-tut-tut-tut-tut-tut as he leans his weight down against the box and presses the trigger with his foot to operate the machine which shakes sand down tight around the metal mould. He heaves the box over, shovels damp sand into the other half, places the core where the molten metal will run in, and once again braces himself against the jolting of the machine to shake down the sand. On the floor he breaks open the box, takes the mould gingerly from the sand, and closes the box again where it lies with a dozen others, ready for furnace day. Looking over his finished moulds Curl Skidmore is depressed. Across the floor the old bloke in blue-grey dungarees has done nineteen. To his left the young foreman has done twenty-three. In theory it is a great job. You work either eight hours a day or as long as it takes to make your quota of moulds, and if you finish your quota early you go home, or if you finish and stay to do more than your quota you get a bonus. But Curl has never yet finished his quota early, and though he has been doing the job full-time for more than a month he doesn't seem to be getting any faster. So instead of arriving home in the afternoon in time to make a start on getting one of his novels down on paper, he is here all day, the sacred scrolls of fiction so shaken and jolted by the machine that there are times when, going over them as he cycles wearily down to the ferry wharf in the evening, he finds them mixed or blurred, one spool running into the other and both fading into an obscurity from which only sleep and the cold early light of morning over the Gulf can rescue them. Furnace day is a better day, swinging the huge ladle over the moulds, pouring the molten iron in the morning and in the afternoon breaking out the casts and admiring them and looking for imperfections. But on furnace day you have also to put up with heat and with the comments of the foreman and the others when the tally is made. It's true that a metal foundry is not an Ivory Tower. It may even be true that a metal foundry is in some sense the Real World and that a university is not. But Curl Skidmore has begun to wonder about that, and about all those who have urged him to get out of the university and discover what the Real World is all about. Melior Farbro, for example, may be in the Real World, but he is not in a metal foundry. Neither is Cecelia Skyways. And it is they and Pat now who talk about books and pictures in the evenings, books read and books to be written, pictures seen and pictures to be painted, while the brilliant young Skidmore, his Takapuna piece forgotten, his novels slipping from and erasing on their spools, nods in his chair and dreams of his machine jolting under him like an angry steer, or of hot metal pouring into his head and setting so that he wakes with his jaw rigid and his teeth grinding as if they have been welded together.

And as for Cecelia Skyways, in the matter of employment hers has never been what is called 'gainful' except for a period of a few months when as a young girl, fresh from Stratford College in the Province of Taranaki and in sight of Mt Egmont, she entered Teachers College and began training for the education service. After that it was downhill all the way and most of the long bad trip is no longer available to her – she can't remember it and doesn't want to remember, since she has learned from her Master, Bodidharma of the Web, that past and future are illusions and there is only the present which is the moment of life. Still sometimes fragments out of that illusory past come back to her, and one she remembers is a scene in which – she doesn't know where or when – a kind doctor in a white coat leans over her bed smiling a kind false smile and asks her name.

'Harpo,' she replies.

'So we're Harpo today are we,' says the kind doctor with his kind false smile. 'And how are we feeling?'

'We're feeling fine,' replies Cecelia. 'Both of us.' And she draws out from beneath the sheet the pair of scissors she has stolen from the sewing room and snips off the kind doctor's tie.

And for Nathan Stockman music has always been his employment and his employment music, because there has always been family money, his father's business selling music and musical instruments, and for him there has been the violin, first learning to play it and then teaching others to play it, and it seems to him now that he has lived inside a cocoon of it, so that even when they didn't have enough to pay off the expensive house Emil designed for them, and when Felice wouldn't go with him to Wellington to take the job that was waiting for him there with the National Orchestra, and the idea came to him ('brilliant', everyone agreed) to open a restaurant, still he thought in terms of music. So it was to be a restaurant where you could eat and listen to him playing the violin – a 'Gipsy violin' the advertisement said, because not everyone with an appetite for good food would have an appetite also for Bach and Mozart. And now the business has collapsed and the house gone up in smoke and the insurance will probably not be paid because there are different stories about who is to blame for the fire. Nathan and Felice have moved into the little two-roomed outhouse flat across the white courtyard from Curl and Pat, and Nathan sits in a deck-chair in the courtyard wondering how much longer the good weather will hold, or he sits down on the sand under the tamarisks, his back against the warm wall, or he plays chess with Curl who has begun to weary of the metal foundry and to take days off work. Not even Felice's sighs and tears give Nathan pleasure any longer. 'I'm unemployed,' he says to himself, and though he keeps promising to put an advertisement in the newspaper to say he is once again available to teach the violin, still he hasn't done it yet, and somewhere underneath his promises there is the thought, 'While the summer lasts, why should I?'

And while Nathan sits alone in his deck-chair, or (at those times when Curl takes the day off) while Nathan and Curl sit out under the cabbage tree playing chess, and while the heavenly notes of the Felicevoice (she has begun to work at it again) come arrowing through the walls of the outhouse bathroom where the plump little sinner has taken herself to practise, Pat Bennett, plain Pat always when she gets on with designated tasks, applies herself at the table looking out across the Gulf (but she doesn't look out) to the folio of designs and sketches and watercolours which is her current assignment as a student at the Elam School of Art, while the furious Mrs Battle, lifting curtain corners and peering through inch-open doors, fumes and frets at a world full of inactivity, a harbour full of unloaded ships, a town full of unimprisoned agitators. 'Oh the spirit of service is dead,' she hisses to herself, step-dragging about in as near as her dead leg will allow to what her iron will requires – the action of pacing up and down. 'Thank God my Charles, at least, is a *worker*.'

And Charles Battle, neat and tight in his uniform, stands eight hours per day, four of a morning shift, four of an afternoon (with turns, when they come due, on the late and the early) in a wooden box, sentry style, at the entrance to the ferry wharf, clipping tickets. Not a ticket escapes him, every ticket gets a clip, even in the rush hour when the ticket-bearers come through and bank up in a hot impatient crowd. 'Snip. Snip-snip. Snip,' goes Charles Battle's punch, and the clippings fly out far and fast with the speed and crispness of the snip. 'Snip. Snip-snip.' Never a ticket missed. Every ticket with a big bold clear-edged tear in its side, nothing blurred or uncertain, every one fatally wounded, never to be used again.

It is possible that intelligent tadpoles reconcile themselves to the inconveniences of their position by reflecting that, though most of them will live and die as tadpoles and nothing more, the more fortunate of the species will one day lose their tails, hop nimbly

65

on to dry land, and croak addresses to their former friends on the virtues by means of which tadpoles of character and capacity can rise to be frogs.

Typed out on a neat card some time during the 1930s and pinned among so many things pinned to the walls of Melior Farbro's studio, this quotation looks down on the ginger-gold head of Cecelia Skyways, on the dark glinting head of Pat Bennett, on the greying but still brown head of Melior Farbro, and on the straight-haired nodding punch-drunk head of Curl Skidmore as they sit in the evening talking about books and pictures. The card has curled up at the edges, it is dusty and fly-spotted, it is long since Melior has read it or given it any thought, and it reminds Cecelia Skyways of the Zen poet Basho's famous haiku about the frog and the pond. Cecelia, it is to be inferred, under instruction from her spider (though it's not quite correct to call it instruction: he neither demands particular work of her nor offers praise nor blame when she does some) has changed her notion of what the best in literature must be. *War and Peace*, she explains, is by definition a false book. No satori (she uses her Master's word for enlightenment) can be sustained for a thousand pages. It can't be sustained for one! So although she is continuing her *Memoirs of a Railway Siding* they are moving more slowly now. She regards them as no more than a limbering up of the mind at the typewriter. Her best efforts are going into poems, five-line tankas, three-line haikus, and each finished poem is transcribed, as the first was, in red and black ink on to a piece of parchment paper and hung from the ceiling of the hut, which she has repainted. Some remain there no more than a day. They are seen to be not after all a true satori, not even a small one. But seven remain, and of these she is sure of four. 'It's my work,' says Cecelia Skyways with a shy ambiguous smile. 'Even the Lady of Shalott was a worker. She was a weaver, wasn't she?'

But she will not show them her poems. Nor does she tell them that the best of them, the one she knows Bodhidharma of the Web regards as her only true satori (though he hasn't said so) is one which came to her in a flash as they sat together and watched the nodding head of Curl (she thought of him as Urlich)

66

Skidmore and noticed that the pale smooth skin of his cheeks and brow was faintly freckled:

> Stream water whispers
> 'Long journey gave you this thirst.
> Drink. Do not build dreams.'

And even a mountain might be said to have a job to do, especially if it should be a mountain in a sea and consequently an island, guarding from the turbulences of open ocean the approaches to a harbour; forming, with the shoreline, a broad channel down which ships pass in and out; rising out of the sea from its broad base with such even and matching angles on either side, closing so geometrically upon the indentation of the volcanic crater at its summit, that it looks sometimes like a cardboard cutout tufted over with fluffy green dabs that are supposed to be trees but are really the work of the architect or stage-designer who created it. Rangitoto: Bloody Sky – recent enough in its eruption for the vegetation among its still unweathered scoria to seem a first generation; possessed of a strange and beautiful and brooding darkness even under the harshest of light; bearer at night on its long arms and outreaches of the winking and flashing lights of the channel; first welcomer to the Gulf of the rising moon; and today, sole possessor of a magic which can detach Mrs Battle momentarily from her sacred rages, so that she leans on the broom with which she has been chastising the verandah and, taken unawares, remembers lying, long ago but not far away, in the grass on a clifftop looking across the Gulf to that same stone composure and seeing among the foreground stalks a spider dancing in front of her nose. Was it, she wondered, the breeze which made the spider dance, or the action of re-rigging its web? Or were there times when spiders forgot to build and to trap and simply danced in the wind for the sake of dancing?

And what a day it is for Mrs Battle to be having such high-flown not to say Skyways thoughts. Because today are blowing squalls of rain across the peninsula from the west. That best of the

67

summer which cannot hold much longer appears all at once to have torn, to have flapped, to have held a moment to its pegs and then to have blown entirely away. Of course the sun will return. There will be good days and bad days, but that security, that sense of certainty, is gone. And with it comes by radio and newsprint the latest on what is called the Strike. Although the watersiders' officials in Wellington have appeared to accept all seven of the Prime Minister's seven points together with the principle of compulsory arbitration it is clear to the Prime Minister (and even clearer to his Minister of Labour Sullivan, who has made it clear to the Prime Minister), that these union officials, wreckers to a man, do not mean what they say, are not to be trusted. And this is confirmed by the Moral Rearmament man who is given time to talk about it on the wireless and by Mrs Battle's tea-leaves turned three times in her upturned cup and by Mrs Battle herself, in person, on the verandah in the squally morning once again chastising its floor with a broom and sweeping down spiderwebs from under the corrugated iron on which the rain beats unmercifully.

Certainly a dog has at least one job to do every day and Rosh (no one thinks of him now as Hiroshima though his date of birth was 6 August 1945) is no exception whether or not the angry camera is hidden in the greenhouse waiting to catch him at it, and in any case today is overcast and not a day for amateur photography.

And even a member of a Parliament which does not meet, a large round one-thousand-a-year man with a medal on his watch-chain allowing him free passage on the railways has something more to do (even if he doesn't do it) than just sit at home in his big brown armchair in his small gloomy panelled study under the damp shadow of Mt Eden, smoking and coughing and reading murder mysteries and feeling that if things go on as they are his political career will have one foot in its grave and the other on a banana skin.

So Ken, and another from the union who is probably called

Fred, are peddling slowly along Ponsonby Road in the rain on grocery delivery bicycles with small wheels and a big square metal frame at the front for the grocery boxes. The bicycles have been lent by a friendly grocer, and the big square white loaves they are delivering to the watersiders' families have been baked by a friendly baker.

'God I would've settled for four and tenpence ha'penny sooner than this,' Fred says, 'but we're not going to get a chance to settle for anything.'

And the boss says, 'Are you responsible for these pamphlets?' and Curl Skidmore says, 'Yes,' and the boss says, 'Do you know they're illegal?' and Curl Skidmore says, 'Yes,' and the boss says, 'Do you know you're the slowest machine moulder in the factory?' and Curl Skidmore says, 'Yes.' So the boss says, 'Yes. Yes. Yes. Three right answers, and you're fired,' and Curl Skidmore says, 'Thank God.' 'Don't thank Him, thank me,' says the boss, and Curl Skidmore says, 'When do I collect my pay?'

FIVE

Sorry, Wrong Dream

Autumn – early autumn – can offer the best Auckland weather, with that windowpane brightness and clearness of air and light that belong to Wellington and the South Island, but with the mildness that belongs to the North. It is, for that season only, mildness without a blurring of edges. The blade is sharp, the water sparkles, the far hills have precise lines and don't melt into one another, and the mind is fresh and alert. So if Chapter Five should be done professionally, by what I've heard called 'a fully paid-up novelist', it might begin as follows:

'Pass me the butter, Cecil,' said Melior.

They were sitting on either side of the counter that separated his kitchen from his studio, and the light of an autumn morning, clear and fresh and mild, played brilliantly upon the ginger-gold mop that was the head of Cecelia Skyways.

'It's what I want,' she said – and clearly she was not referring to the butter, which she held abstractedly, so that it wobbled in the air between them and he did not know whether or not he should simply reach out and take it from her erratic fingers. 'It's what I've wanted since I first saw him.'

Melior decided to take the butter. 'It's what he wants too,' he said; and he, no more than Cecelia had been, was referring to the butter. 'Of course he hasn't said so directly. But whenever he talks about you, Cecil – believe me, his eyes light up, he says you're beautiful, he gets excited. I know the signs.' Melior laughed. 'It makes me quite jealous.'

'Well . . .' She shrugged, watching the older man buttering his toast. 'It needn't be anything more than a visit. If we could just spend an hour or two together . . .'

'Precisely,' Melior agreed. 'If nothing comes of it no harm's been done.' But you could see by the look in his eye that he did not suppose for a moment that nothing would come of it. Melior Farbro knew, was obsessed with, never stopped turning over in his mind, what tinder boxes the young were, and he did not believe a meeting could take place out there in the hut in the wilderness of his back garden, a meeting between two such brilliant creatures as Cecelia (he thought of her as Cecil) and Urlich (he thought of him as Curl) without there being some kind of conflagration. If that was what she wanted, young Skidmore would want it too, and good luck to them both.

'And you're sure,' she said. 'I mean about the poems. You don't think it might seem . . .' She hesitated. 'Trumped up?'

He spread his crumb-covered fingers, palm upward. 'Cecil darling, it's not trumped up. If you've begun to write poems in a new style you need someone to read and to comment. And much better when you're young to get the opinion of a contemporary.'

She smiled under her aureole of hair. 'I think you're right, Melior.' And for the first time she looked as if she was fully convinced.

This was not the first time it had been discussed. For weeks now they had . . .

And so the narrative, having begun concretely and dramatically, with the butter to lend authenticity, and with dialogue which did not fully explain itself and thus had the flavour of the real, would now track back and fill in what had not been explained, how Cecelia had admitted to her obsession with Curl Skidmore and to a wish for a kind of experience which the 'convent' hadn't permitted, and how Melior, excited at something which seemed to offer the chance of a vicarious participation in the rages of youthful sexuality, had probed and prompted and encouraged and finally devised a simple plan by which the two young writers could be left alone together to sort out their feelings and wishes in respect of one another. Such an account would be thoroughly professional. But perhaps the character of Cecelia Skyways, lying as it does a little to the east or perhaps to the south of that norm of the normally abnormal which is the province of professional fiction, might in any case slip through every net put out for it, even one so all-purpose and capacious as the morning breakfast table and the opening gambit, 'Pass me the butter'.

Bodhidharma had offered no ordinary objection to the plan. He had (if only silently) approved her haiku in which the stream had said:

> Long journey gave you this thirst.
> Drink. Do not build dreams.

It was not her slaking of a thirst he objected to. But he offered her many warnings against the building of dreams. And he reminded her of the answer of that Master who was asked for the inner secret of Zen Buddhism and replied, 'When I am hungry I eat, when I am thirsty I drink, when I am tired I lie down and sleep.' This being so the Master did not dream of eating, did not long for water nor yearn for sleep, did not think of them when he was neither eating, drinking nor sleeping, but lived inside the action or the contemplation of the moment. So Cecelia lived inside her *Memoirs of a Railway Siding* while she wrote them, lived inside the action of gardening while she raked the unplanted soil and heaved into position five large scoria stones in the corner Melior had allowed her to make her own, lived inside practical puzzles and their solutions while she worked at making a windharp to hang in her Zen garden, lived inside her eyes and her ears and her tongue and her nostrils and her skin and her joints while she sat cross-legged in contemplation. But still the dreams and the questioning could not be entirely eliminated. 'Should I worry about Pat?' she asked Bodhidharma and he replied, 'Don't be irrelevant.' 'Should I worry about Pat?' she repeated, and he replied, 'Don't be insincere.' 'Should I worry about Pat?' she asked a third time, and he replied, 'Don't be insolent.' So the April day and the April days passed and the plan which was not allowed to be the substance of a dream was hatched and Cecelia Skyways raked and wrote and squatted and strung and sometimes

72

achieved in seventeen syllables or in a moment something her
Master did not object to her calling satori.

The April sun is in the white yard and out on the blue water.
Under the cabbage tree Nathan Stockman is tuning his violin,
playing scales and exercises, tuning again. Through the walls of
the outhouse bathroom come the arrows of the Felicevoice. At
the table that looks out over the Gulf sits plain Pat Bennett not
looking out, her black waves falling over her beautiful face as
she works in pencil and in crayon. On the steps down into the
yard Curl sits with a pad on his knee, writing. On either side of
him there are books he ought to be reading now he has made a
late enrolment at the university. But an idea has come to him
and he is writing. He is striking off brilliant images. He is
writing with wit. Oh how buoyant he can be on the page, how
incomparably deft and swift and sharp-shafted when he is so
unhappy, so weighed down with gloom that his limbs when
he moves them feel like dead weights. Up there sits the
impenetrable Pat Bennett, her puzzle, wrapped in dark shiny
hair and olive skin, insoluble even to herself. For three days she
has worked at her assignment, locked in one of her selves, the
deepest, the innermost box of her, which is neither Maori nor
French and might contain ice or fire but does not express itself
in the ordinary language of civility and affection. It might be
the Celt in her, and it comes out in long silences and short
angers, and through the tip of her pencil on to the pages of the
sketchbook. To put it more simply in the language Nathan
Stockman applies to her from a genial distance, Pat (he thinks
of her as Patagonia) is working well and while she's in the vein
she shouldn't be disturbed. Curl doesn't disturb her. He has
spent the morning trying and failing to make up for lectures
missed by reading books which he finds boring and half believes
(the belief is suppressed) are stupid as well. They are books on
books, recommended by a kindly professor helping him make
up lost ground. At intervals he has been going to the kitchen to
make himself yet another white bread and peanut butter
sandwich. The peanut butter he stole yesterday from the
grocer's shelves, because he is going through peanut butter so

fast he feels he can't go on paying for it every time. Now and then it will have to come free. He thinks his sexual energies are somehow related to his consumption of peanut butter and his energies just now, even if (or perhaps because) largely frustrated, are high. So his mind runs from the silence at the table-looking-out, to the shrieks and whoops and carollings from the outhouse bathroom where the plump white enticing Felice who seems wholly recovered from the disaster with the cook (referred to in the private language exchanged by Curl and Pat as the Frying Pan who preceded the Fire) is putting her larynx through its paces. She sings, Nathan plays, both are enlivened by Nathan's plan which is that they should go abroad and start again, in London. She will sing at Covent Garden or Sadlers Wells, even if it is no more than the most insignificant part in the chorus. He will find a place in some dusty corner of one of the London orchestras. They will start at the bottom of the ladder and they will climb it together. Everything that seemed to hold them, the few real things and the many intangible ones, have gone up in smoke, vanished with the fire. If the insurance pays out, that will clear the mortgage and leave them something for fares and getting started in London. If it doesn't, they will sell the land to clear the mortgage and Nathan's father will lend them money for fares. That decision has been discussed this morning to and fro across the yard. It has made the air alive around the cabbage tree, it has set moving through the blue April weather the ineffable currents to which at times Curl Skidmore is the helpless windharp. And there is for Curl a kind of therapy in giving in to them, letting them blow through him, sounding his strings. As long as he continues to write as those currents dictate the misery of the moment is set aside. It is only as he lifts his head from the page that the leaden echo sounds again and he is forced to scramble back into the kitchen for another peanut butter sandwich. And then down into the yard comes Rosh, scampering around and back and forth to greet Nathan, to greet Curl, to greet Nathan again, his tail wagging so hard it curves his body sideways and forces him to stop in mid-run and bite at it to bring it under control. Rosh is the front-runner announcing another arrival.

74

Behind him comes Melior Farbro, his rucksack heavy with vegetables and fruit. He is like Santa Claus, plunging a hand into the rucksack and discovering what's there. 'This one for you, Nathan. These for Curl. Oh and *this*' (a long green cucumber) 'for Felice. A pumpkin for all of you – and maybe a bit for Mrs Battle? And share these around. And this apple – it's the first of this lot – just one – isn't it a beauty? – this is for darling Pat, of course. We in the visual arts, we have to support one another.' So darling Pat is deflected a moment from her work and handed the apple up through the window from the yard with the others looking on – a presentation, and Felice who has come out of the bathroom to receive her cucumber applauds, and Nathan calls for a speech, but Pat's mind is somewhere else, back there on the sketchpad sheets, and she bites into her apple as if it had been any old apple and walks back along the verandah to her table, tossing the hair back from her brow. And now Melior is near the bottom of his sack, among the root vegetables, and it's here he mentions, head down, voice a trifle nervous, that he has a message for Curl, a little problem, something that needs sorting out, and Curl, leaving his books and his manuscripts heaped up on the steps, crosses the lawn with him and together they step out for a brief chat and a stroll along the sand.

When Curl returns from the beach he finds Nathan crouching in the yard chopping up the big green-grey pumpkin with an axe. Felice is bending over him, watching. Pat has come into the yard. She's standing looking up at the rattling spiky leaves of the cabbage tree moving in the breeze against a blue sky. Curl comes up behind her, hesitating. He wants to put his hand into hers, which is resting, palm outward, against her buttock, but he's nervous she might pull away angrily. 'I'm afraid of her,' he thinks. It's something new.

'I've murdered it,' Nathan says, looking down at the pumpkin scattered in pieces over the concrete. While they look down at it Curl tells them what Melior wanted. Cecelia is writing new poems, she needs help with them, would welcome his opinion, thinks his eye, and more particularly his ear, might

75

be useful. Pat laughs. She says nothing. Curl is conscious he has brought out the news a little pompously, pleased to be asked to help.

He looks to discover in Pat's face the meaning of the laugh, but she's looking up at the sky again.

Cecelia has simplified her life. She has simplified the hut. She still sleeps on a bed and writes at a table, but the floor is covered with matting, the walls are plain, and from the ceiling hang the scrolls on which her poems are copied, moving this way and that with the movements of air. Through the open door can be seen that path she has cleared and the garden she has made, five scoria stones set in an unplanted rectangle of soil, the soil surface raked into swirling patterns, backed by an unfinished palisade of Melior's tomato stakes and watched over (this is her invention, not sanctioned by her Master, though he hasn't objected either) by the windharp. Arriving at her door Curl Skidmore feels shy of her, and more so when he detects that she is shy of him. But he follows her directions and sits cross-legged opposite her while she makes tea. Lacking a charcoal burner she uses a primus to heat the water. It is a pottery teapot she uses, and she pours the pale tea into pottery cups.

She asks about his writing and he tells her of the idea he has had this morning on the steps and how much he has done and how well it has gone. It is about Rangitoto.

'Your Rangitoto piece,' she says, smiling faintly.

He is trying not to look at her knees. She has drawn up her skirt to make it easier to sit cross-legged, and sitting opposite her he is aware that her knees are neat and round and pale and that between them there is a dark space into which it would be improper to stare.

She is saying it's kind of him to come. She has asked Melior to ask him if he would. She has so much enjoyed talking to him in the evenings at Melior's, or not talking to him – it's much the same, doesn't he think? Communication, and silent communication. But sometimes it's hard to get from one to the other. What people say aloud and what they say silently doesn't always match, and mostly that doesn't matter but aren't there times

76

when it does and when it's as well to make the effort to bring them into line?

She is joined in her monologue by a cicada. Curl can't see it but he can tell by the sound it makes that it's big and black and old, one of those cicadas that survive into the autumn and show up on sunny days. It goes k-za k-za k-za k-za k-za with a clicking noise at the end of each burst of sound. Cecelia's voice continues, clear and pure. Curl sinks in on himself and his consciousness, wandering here and there, inside the hut, out through the half-open door, comes back always to that dark centre into which he doesn't look. Floating in him like a dream is the action of reaching gently forward into that darkness. As he looks down the path to the scoria stones set in their raked bed, as he listens to the sound of the cicada abstracting itself, k-za k-za k-za k-za k-za k-za, as he hears the voice of Cecelia Skyways, it too becoming pure sound, meaningless, that dream of action repeats itself, a simple reaching forward to place his hand there at the centre of things.

Cross-legged the two of them sit, face to face, the path out there seeming to shimmer, the scoria stones to float like islands in their raked sea, while overhead the scroll poems sail like kites or like clouds. The muscles of Curl Skidmore's arm are already under instruction, the hand, the fingers are in slow motion, the dreamaction is on the point of translating itself into the sphere of time and of history, when the revolt occurs. Curl stands abruptly knocking the teapot on to the matting where it lies leaking a puddle of amber liquid. Cecelia falls silent. So does her brother the cicada, while Curl, his voice rather louder than necessary, begins to talk about her poems. Melior has said she wants an opinion, some help, an outside view. Well, for what his opinion's worth, he thinks they're good. Yes. And they look lovely on the scrolls. Style. Beautiful clarity. Nice images. Nice ideas. Of course there's a problem with form, isn't there? The Japs can get away with that short snappy form – he supposes it's because their script is ideogrammic, so it has a pictorial dimension that gets lost in Western alphabetical writing. Pretty easy for the whole thing to slide into a sort of pastiche of oriental wisdom – doesn't she think? Enigmatic wise words. A mind

puzzle and a bash on the head with the master's pipe and bingo!
– you have enlightenment. He doesn't know whether you can
escape from the problem of Western verse form all that easily.
It's refreshing though. No doubt about it! Worth having a shot
at. This one, for example:

> Stream water whispers
> 'Long journey gave you this thirst.
> Drink! Do not build dreams.'

– delightful! You can't get that kind of simplicity into a
conventional Western poem . . .

And while he offers her these opinions off the top of his head
Curl Skidmore is pacing up and down listening to an inner voice
that is saying, 'Oh Jesus,' and, 'Oh shit,' and, 'Can't we get out
of here?'

He stops talking at last because he's getting no response.
Cecelia has remained where she was, cross-legged on the floor.
She sits very still and quite silent and when he allows himself a
direct glance at her face he sees it set hard, like one of those
scoria stones out there. It's not even anger he sees in it but
something worse.

'Better go,' he mumbles, looking at his watch. 'Time to be
off. Do you . . . Could you . . . Is there . . .'

But the stone face doesn't, couldn't, and there isn't, not even
for a second. He leaves her there and hurries away, and when
Melior Farbro stops him along the path, his elbow nudging, his
eyebrows going up and down like a blind, Curl Skidmore isn't
able to do more than mumble incoherently that he's had tea
thanks, and yes they've talked about her new poems, and maybe
she isn't very well.

The sound of her door slamming shut makes them both start.
Curl says goodbye and walks back towards the beach.

In the hut, behind the door slammed shut, Bodhidharma of the
Web has silently assumed the voice of the mother of Cecelia
Skyways:

I told you I warned you but what's the use no one ever listens
to me I don't know why I even care I don't know why I bother I

tell a person a thing and do they listen no they don't no dreams I
said don't build on it I said if it happens fine I said if it doesn't
there's no skin off anyone's nose not yours not mine not his but
do you take any notice do you listen no you don't you just go your
own way you let things get out of proportion and then you wonder why you get hurt I don't know you drive me to distraction
you really do what's the use of me trying to help it's just a waste
of effort on my part I might as well save my breath to cool my
porridge as my father used to say mind you in those days things
were different and when an adult spoke we listened there was
some respect then I can tell you and so there should be and if
there wasn't our parents wanted to know the reason why anyway I blame myself I should have said no stay away from him
he's not worth a tin of fish I could see that at a glance but oh you
just had to have your own way didn't you you just had to go after
him you were always one for looking at the boys don't think I
didn't notice I've got eyes in my head despite what some of you
think I wasn't born yesterday miss and it hasn't gone past me
unnoticed but as for that Skidmore creature I could have told
you you were wasting your time it wouldn't surprise me at all if
he was one of those you-know-whats and I think your prize
Melior Farbro might be a cut of the same cloth even if he has got
a very good vegy garden which I'd be the first to concede being
one to give credit where it's due but that doesn't alter the fact
that this is a weird mob you've got yourself mixed up with and
do you wonder people think there's something wrong with your
head if you let yourself be influenced by that sort of person
instead of taking notice of your own mother well I'm not going
to go on about it it's true I've worked my fingers to the bone for
you and got very little thanks but it's not going to continue
sooner or later the worm will turn you should have realized that
I'm not going to make a doormat of myself for the pleasure of
the likes of you my girl so let this be a warning to you and if you
go near that Skidmore thing again I won't just stop your pocket
money I'll get your father to tan the hide off of you so help me I
will . . .

Meanwhile in the verandah flat Curl had been doing his best

against odds to pace up and down which was what he needed to do if his feelings were to be relieved while he talked. It was not just the narrowness of the verandah that made it difficult but that strange slope in the floor from the level at the kitchen end to the level at the end where the table looked out to beach and sea. But he made the effort and kept moving, if not pacing, up and down while he let off steam and tried to explain and while Aorewa (she was wearing a flax headband and she had painted a moko with eyebrow pencil on her chin) sat at the table and looked out and listened. Curl was in pain, he was in stitches, he winced and shuddered to the bottom of his being it had been so awful, it had gone so disastrously wrong, and if Ao could only have seen Cecelia's face when he was leaving . . .

But Aorewa made him tell it all in order, he had to begin at the beginning, he had to remember what he had said, what Cecelia had said, what he'd thought, what he thought she'd thought, step by step until the moment when he had stood up knocking over the teapot. And because she was not plain Pat, nor wild Patagonia at this moment, but Aorewa, calm, measured, inscrutable and oracular, he found himself telling her the truth he might have expected to conceal, that he'd wanted to put his hand under Cecelia's skirt, that he'd had the feeling she wouldn't have minded at all. And Aorewa made him complete the story, remembering in as much detail as he could what he'd said about the poems and how Cecelia had responded or not responded and how he'd felt during those final moments before leaving. So he got it all straight in his head and told it all honestly to Aorewa who sat staring out to sea after he'd finished and then turned and looked at him with an expression that was faintly amused and a shade reproachful.

'You should have gone right ahead,' she said. 'You'd gone too far to pull back.'

'But what about . . .' he faltered.

'I would have murdered you,' she said.

'Well then . . .' he began again.

'You needn't have told me,' she said.

He looked at her enquiringly.

'But don't try it,' she said, 'because if you do – I'll know.'

There was no sound at all from the hut. Melior had called her for dinner in his usual offhand way, trying to behave as if nothing had happened, but there was no response. Finally he'd taken a plate out to her and tapped gently on the door and called to her and said wouldn't she like to eat something, and when there was still no reply, only silence on the other side of the door, he'd left it on the step saying it was there if she wanted it. Later again he'd heard a noise and gone out to find Rosh licking the plate clean.

'Clear off you little bugger,' Melior shouted, throwing a stick at Rosh who darted away and then trotted down the path to the front gate casting looks back over his shoulder. Now it was late and the lamp was lit in the hut so she was alive and there was nothing to be done but sit quiet and let time sort things out. What had gone wrong in there? Had Curl gone too far too fast? Had he forgotten she'd spent five years in a convent?

And at the same time that Melior worried about it the thought set some of the blue movies running inside his head, starring himself and little Ken, and Cecil and Curl, the stars chasing one another around like cartoon figures so that his imaginings mixed into and merged with his new paintings as he drifted asleep, his light still on and a book propped open against his knees. He might have slept five minutes or it might have been half an hour when he was awakened by a bang in the kitchen and footsteps. He lay still, alert. It wasn't her usual walk or movements but he knew it was Cecil, and he caught just a glimpse of her as she passed his open door and went on out into the garden. His back door, then the door of the hut, slammed shut and there was silence.

Melior got out of bed and went into the kitchen. The middle had been torn out of a loaf of white bread which lay on the counter. The milk jug was lying on its side on the sink bench and the meat-safe door was open. Well, at least she didn't intend to starve and that was something. Across the room he noticed a gap on his bookshelves where the two volumes of *War and Peace* should have been.

Bread, milk and Tolstoy, Melior thought. She's well supplied. And he returned to his bed. In the early hours of the morning he woke again and looked out. The lamp was still burning in her hut.

At the sound of the first bird Cecelia looked up from her book. She was not sitting cross-legged on the floor. She was lounging on her bed, almost aggressively lounging. 'If I had a box of chocolates,' she told her Master in the web, 'I'd be eating them but I haven't so I'm dreaming of eating them – chocolates with soft centres that do terrible things to your teeth.'

There was a faint brush of light in the sky above the garden trees. The first bird had been followed very quickly by the second and the third.

'That's the third bird,' said Cecelia Skyways – and she tried the statement again in what she imagined to be an Irish accent ('That's the t'orrd borrd') and then in Kiwi vernacular ('Thet's the theerd beard').

Now all over the suburb they were starting up. 'Hear them,' Cecelia said to her Master. 'I wonder how many of them are birds that eat spiders. How wud ya loik ta bay ayten boy a borrd. Do they stroik terror inta yrr horrt?'

Bodhidharma seemed to look at her from his web. The sky was growing lighter, the birds kept up their noise.

'How would you like to die, spider?' asked Cecelia Skyways. 'I think you're afraid of dying. I only have to stick a finger into your web and you go round in circles like a mad thing. You see what I'm reading don't you? *War and Peace*. No satori here. No enlightenment in a work of a thousand pages. As you so rightly taught me, it's hard enough to keep it up for five lines. But I'm enjoying it. It's great. It's a comfortable grave and I'm burying myself. And don't start preaching because if you do I might ask how a worthy spirit like yourself got trapped inside the body of a daddy-longlegs. I was wondering about that just yesterday when I read about the Zen monk that got turned into a fox. One of his pupils asked whether the enlightened man was subject to the laws of causation and he answered No and got turned into a fox for arrogance and clinging to absolutes. Something like that happen to you, hmm? Question: Is the enlightened man subject to the laws of causation? Answer: The enlightened man is at one with the laws of causation. You'll know that next time, won't you? You'll remember that please. I'm at one with the laws of causation and at peace with the universe because I'm reading a book with no satori and dreaming of chocolates. How about that, Master? And I've decided not to feed you to the borrds – you know why? Because it might let you out sooner. This might be your last turn as a spider. Is that why you're so full of yourself about not being afraid? You're just waiting to die so you can get back to being a man again – but they might make you a woman. Ever thought of that? A thin-skinned hysterical female. But don't worry. They have all kinds of drugs these days. And machines. Electricity. They'll straighten you out. They'll have you good as gold in no time, boy.'

Melior called her for breakfast and when she didn't come he ate his own and settled to his cartoon series. His worries about Cecelia vanished into the technical problems of how to deal with the continuing onrush of his idea which was so strange even to himself, so unlike anything he'd done before. At the usual time he broke off to make himself coffee. There was no sound from the hut, the typewriter was silent, the air empty of the flying words of Cecelia Skyways, and Melior wondered would she go back to it now or was that silence the end of her *Memoirs*. He called her for coffee but there was no reply. He walked to the letterbox at the gate, worrying, because the worry flooded back as soon as he put down his pens and brushes.

'And I haven't shed a tear, not one,' lied Cecelia Skyways, who had looked through the gap in her curtains and seen Melior coming back from the gate. 'That's pretty good for me don't you agree Body? Maybe you've done me some good after all. I used to be known as the Floodgates. Only had to think about crying and out it came. Probably the electricity that fixed it. Wonderful drying stuff. Dehydration of the tear ducts. Just what the doctor ordered.'

In her hands as she spoke she had one of the scrolls that had hung from the ceiling. She read it aloud:

83

Far away I glimpsed
The blue Waitakere Range.
Shall I arrive there
Ever? At least I know now
The direction I must take.

'Young Skidmore's right,' she said, tearing the scroll
carefully in half and then in half again. 'There's a feeling of
thinness without the whatsits. Ideograms. Curl's right. You
orientals need your ideograms. You can't match us for texture.'
And she quoted:

A bow-shot from her bower-eaves
He rode between the barley sheaves
The sun came dazzling through the leaves
And flamed upon the brazen greaves
        Of bold Sir Lancelot.
A red-cross knight for ever kneel'd
To a lady in his shield
That sparkled on the yellow field
        Beside remote Shalott.

She left the web, she left the loom,
She made three paces thro' the room,
She saw the water-lily bloom,
She saw the helmet and the plume,
        She looked down to Camelot.
Out flew the web and floated wide;
The mirror crack'd from side to side,
'The curse is come upon me,' cried
        The Lady of Shalott.

'The curse came upon her, see, because she was supposed to
stick to her weaving and look at things second-hand in the
mirror. She wasn't supposed to look people square in the eye or
take handfuls of their flesh or listen to them read their poetry.
She knew the rules. She asked for it. She had it coming . . .'
And because Melior had come out into the garden again she
suddenly pushed her window wide open and threw out Volume

One of *War and Peace* so it landed spreadeagled and bent in the dust at his feet. He was startled.

'What's this Cecil?' he said, looking up at the window.

'Finished Vol. One,' she shouted, in a harsh voice. And she slammed the window shut.

'The curse is come upon me,' cried
The Lady of Shalott,

she quoted again. 'I used to know an American girl who called her periods the Curse. When I was at High School we called our periods Alfred because of a poem by Coleridge – *Kubla Khan*. Do you know it, Body? It goes:

Where Alph the sacred river ran
Through caverns measureless to man
Down to a sunless sea.

Have I told you my favourite quotation from Coleridge – I mean apart from *Kubla Khan*? It's here somewhere . . .'

She reached under her bed to the little pile of books she kept there and opened one of them at a marked page.

'It goes like this,' she said. And she read:

'If to destroy the reality of all that we actually behold be idealism, what can be more egregiously so than the system of modern metaphysics, which banishes us to a land of shadows, surrounds us with apparitions, and distinguishes truth from illusion only by the majority of those who dream the same dream? "I asserted that the world was mad," exclaimed poor Lee, "and the world said that I was mad, and confound them, they out-voted me!"'

She looked up from the book and saw that her spider was gyrating.

It was late in the afternoon, the long shadows from the tomato stakes were slanting across the raked swirls in the sea of Cecelia Skyways' garden, and her scoria islands were darkening like Rangitoto, when the door of the hut was pushed open without a knock or a call. It was Melior carrying a bowl of hot soup and he

85

found her struggling in the half light with Volume Two of *War and Peace*.

'Cecil you're not turning me away,' he said. 'You're going to eat something.'

But she showed no sign of resisting. 'I'm so tired,' she said, 'I think I'm going to die, Melior.'

And she lay there on the bed, propped up on pillows, and let him feed her with a spoon.

'Better?' he asked when she had finished, and she put an arm around his shoulder and leaned forward so her head rested against his throat.

'Sorry,' she said. He felt her tears against his skin and he patted her back and ran his fingers through her curls.

'What happened, Cecil?' he asked.

She shook her head. 'Nothing.'

'But,' he said.

'Nothing,' she repeated. 'Nothing happened.'

There was the silence of the moment it took for him to absorb what this meant, and that she wasn't just refusing to tell him, and then, 'Oh Jasper,' he said. 'I never thought of *that*.'

SIX

The Comic Strip

What made Melior Farbro dream his cartoon series? Does the artist foretell, or does his dream create the reality? Why in the ten weeks since he began his series has New Zealand turned itself into a comic strip? Here are men who are not allowed to work and who are told they are on strike. Here are seven points the union leaders must accept before the Government will talk to them and when they accept the seven points they are told they do not accept them sincerely. Here is a population agreeing that it must be denied any statement of the case against the Government so that democracy may be preserved. Here is the closure of halls and the proscription of marches and meetings in the name of free speech. Here is a cartoon strip Prime Minister supported by a cartoon strip Minister of Labour who sings solo and duo and in concert with all the newspaper editors of the nation. Here is a Parliament that has not met for five months and when it does may reasonably be expected to declare that its period of inactivity has enhanced democracy. And while at home a Government is preserving democracy without the aid of Parliament, abroad the little yellow men who wish to destroy it are advancing in what are called 'human waves' which prove that, like rats, they are not human at all and don't mind dying.

So Melior Farbro in his morning world, honoured for canvases and watercolours of old houses, rural landscapes, and city down-and-outers, finds himself reducing the near and the far equally to the clash of bright simple figures in bold colours out of whose mouths issue speech balloons of rhetorical idiocy as they zap and pow their way towards Freedom, Truth, Justice and Democracy. And the worse the world gets, and the more solemn and depressed Melior feels about it, the more extravagant his cartoons become, so he can't stop himself from laughing out loud at them as he stands back to look at what he has done; and the more they make him laugh the more disconcerted he becomes at the thought of what his friends (never mind the enemies) will think of them. 'How long can this go on,' he asks himself, hiding his latest cartoon away so visitors won't see what he is working at. 'Isn't it time I got on to something serious?' But whatever his intellect tells him his imagination won't let him be free of the series. Next morning it presents him with another irresistible idea – and another, and another. The colours harden and brighten, the faces become more contorted, the figures more extreme.

And Ken Blayburn stuffs the trousers that got red paint spilled on them into the culvert in the gully below Mrs Hinchinghorn's boarding house and climbs back to his outhouse room to hear the news, thinking, 'It'd take more than a plaster dog to do real harm to Roy Belsham's thick skull' – but worrying just the same . . .

And Rosh, sleeping beside his calm deaf mother, twitches and jumps in his sleep because someone has turned up the radio extra loud . . .

And Mrs Battle, jumping with excitement in her rocker, shouts, 'Quieten down you fool,' to her dear son Charles who is beating the saucepan again, marching up and down in the dark of the verandah . . .

And out in the Gulf the island of Rangitoto spreads itself darkly and is silent and though its beacons flash on and off none of them on this night can be said to wink . . .

And Melior Farbro, listening to the radio, laughs, thinking of his cartoon series, and tells himself, 'It's all catching up with me, I'll have to take it further . . .'

And 'My word,' thinks the Prime Minister, and 'Oh yes,' he thinks and he thinks 'How true,' listening to himself on the radio in his office in Parliament Buildings . . .

And 'Evil' taps the *Herald* leader writer, and 'Violence', and 'Evil' again and 'Intimidation', and 'Terrorism', and 'Gangsterism', shifting from buttock to buttock uncomfortably in his seedy office thinking, 'When the hell are they going to issue me with a new chair?' . . .

Never before, says the Prime Minister, who likes as many things as possible to be happening for the first time, Never before has he broadcast to the people of New Zealand with a greater sense of responsibility or with a deeper sense of public duty. When he took the oath of office he swore to do his duty to his country and its people. Tonight he is honouring his pledge to king and country, because as everyone must know, the industrial crisis which has gripped the nation for ten weeks has taken a turn for the worse, a very grave turn. A determined effort has been made to overthrow the Government by force. The Government has sought by every means to overcome . . . It has shown patience in . . . Now a dastardly attempt . . . Explosives . . . Miraculous that no serious loss of life . . . Who would have dreamed that in this lovely land of ours . . . And what else have these desperate and evil men . . . in the dead of night . . . an innocent worker who only wanted to . . . beaten into . . . maimed . . . counter-action called for . . . call on all men of . . . Civil Emergency Organization . . . in every city and town . . . Mayors and Councils everywhere . . . armed against . . . the nation must . . . pray that in . . . strike back . . . combat terrorism . . . rule of law . . . any step necessary . . .

And the night sky, closing over, covers like a hand
The barbaric yawn of a young and wrinkled land
thinks Melior Farbro, though the lines are not his but Rex Fairburn's, and it is now not night but morning, the morning after the Prime Minister's speech, which like the morning after a session of heavy drinking has left a day threatening and thunderous, with rumbles at the corners of the sky and as yet only scatters of rain. But despite himself Melior's limp as he moves away from his drawing board is springy, and though more than once he crosses the room intending to make himself coffee or tea, he keeps returning to look again at what he has

done, and each time, against the drift of his own anxiety and his own sense that this is not after all what his public expects of a serious artist, his face breaks into smiles. It's good, he thinks, catching for a moment a quite objective sense of the hardness, the harshness, the movement, the boldness of colour and the extravagance of his latest cartoon; and he does a little skip away from the drawing board and this time makes it all the way across the studio floor to the kettle which he fills and puts on the stove. From out in the garden comes the sound of the machine of Cecelia Skyways, less fluent now, less subject to flurries and surges, but tapping bravely on with her *Memoirs of a Railway Siding*. Now the gate latch clicks and the typewriter in the hut stops as it always does when there is a stranger on the path and Melior looks out to see Police Sergeant Robinson from the Takapuna Station. There is a moment in which Melior's stomach lurches remembering the tone of the Prime Minister's speech and his insistence that the police must feel free to take 'whatever steps are necessary'.

'So soon?' says Melior, as Sergeant Robinson lifts his big fist to knock at the open door. 'I can't say you're welcome, Sergeant, but you're just in time for a cup of tea' – and he points to the two cups on the counter one of which was intended for Cecelia who he knows won't come now there's a stranger in the house. So the sergeant settles down on the stool on the studio side of the counter while Melior, not rushing matters, warms the pot and fills it and puts a cosy over it and puts it between them alongside the two cups and takes the stool on the kitchen side opposite the sergeant. And while this Western version of Cecelia Skyways' tea ceremony is being elaborated they are exchanging desultory and laconic Kiwi chat touching on the threats that are being uttered this morning at the dark corners of the sky and the likelihood that these, properly translated out of the language of the gods in which they are delivered, mean rain in the afternoon. How this may affect Melior's garden is also mentioned which in turn provides an opportunity for enquiries and responses revealing that Sergeant Robinson's garden has been neglected since the advent of what are referred to as 'the troubles', which have loaded a great deal of extra work

90

upon all the 'uniformed services'. And at this the sergeant delivers himself of several statements about troublemakers and wreckers and spoilers and gutless boobies who've never done afairday'sworkforafairday'spay. But the broadside is also reassuring because Melior (pouring now in long spouts which he lengthens and shortens, drawing the pot up towards the ceiling) feels that if the visit had anything to do with the Emergency Regulations the sergeant would have been more circumspect, would have shown a little cunning and conceal-ment. So there is a slight thaw on the kitchen side of the counter and Melior ventures the opinion that there are two sides to every question, even the waterfront dispute, to which the sergeant assents only adding however with reference to Walter Nash, the Leader of the Opposition, and with a turn of metaphor that takes Melior by surprise, that you can't stand on both sides of a barbed wire fence without endangering your balls. So the tea is sipped and then slurped and the sergeant who has troubles with false teeth dunks his round-wine biscuit in the cup before sucking it down. At the corners of the world the gods repeat themselves, and there is a perceptible darkening of the sky.

But it is not for nothing Sergeant Robinson has come and not for a cup of tea either much as it is appreciated and so to get down to the brass tacks of it because his plate is very full today he tells the painter he is making routine enquiries about a missing person whose name is Dawn Clegg and who has escaped. Well Melior hasn't seen Dawn Clegg, doesn't know her, hasn't heard of her, and wonders why the sergeant should think he has.

It's just, the sergeant explains, that someone answering her description has been seen about in this neighbourhood – and he pushes across the counter a slightly bent-edged and tattered photograph of Cecelia Skyways. And it is just at this moment Melior notices with a nervous rush of blood to the face, now compounded by the photograph, that he has left his latest cartoon exposed, and there it is, twenty-one inches by fifteen in hard bright colours and dashing strokes, a comic strip madman recognizably Sidney George Holland beating the shadows with a broom and with a speech bubble yet to be filled issuing from his mouth. So the two recognitions strike Melior together, that out there in the hut is Cecelia to be concealed and across the room in full view should the sergeant turn about to look at it is the cartoon; and it's the desire to cover the cartoon that predominates over the other anxiety which is also, however, acute. So Melior picks up the photograph of Dawn Clegg, pretending to take it into a better light, and crosses the room trying to make himself broad enough so the sergeant won't be able to see through or around him, and before looking at it in the light from the window he contrives to flip down the cartoon and fold away the drawing board as if it had been an obstruction in his path.

No, he assures the sergeant, he has never seen her. And what is she wanted for?

Oh it's not a criminal matter, the sergeant explains. She hasn't escaped from jail. It's not a prison that's wanting her back but a – er hospital. A . . . Yes, that's it. A *mental* hospital. The bin. And no, in answer to that, he couldn't rightly say she was dangerous, though it's said she once attacked or threatened a doctor with a pair of scissors. She's no real threat to the public but for her own good she needs to be locked away, she needs treatment. These folk are always happier in the hands of experts . . .

Melior is anxious to be rid of him now and he is contriving at the same time to talk and to end the talk. The sergeant is down off his stool and saying he'll be on his way and Melior, not hurrying it but not delaying either, ushers him to the door while assuring him that he'll keep a watch out for this person and let the station know should he catch sight of her. The sergeant is thanking him for the cup of tea and the chat, and a flurry of rain is blowing this way and that while the gods flap their thunder curtains in the wings of the sky, and there is not the faintest movement of the curtains over Cecelia's window and not the faintest tap of her typewriter keys as Melior steers the sergeant to the gate and watches him adjusting his cycle clips around the cuffs of his trousers and wobbling away down the road.

Melior breathes, a deep breath, then he turns and walks quickly to the hut.

Curl Skidmore is walking on the sand with Rosh, watching the dark edges of the sky that flap and groan and the pale white light that seems implausibly to drive in patches among stationary layers of cloud. He is sad again, he's mostly sad these days, he accuses himself of wallowing in it. Slowly the novels in his head seem to be fading and he sometimes wonders whether they were ever really there or whether they are a confidence trick he has played on himself and on the world to make himself and Pat, and Melior and Cecelia, and Jim and June, and now Nathan and Felice, believe he's a writer, a real writer with a brilliant future.

Now Rosh has lost his stick, it's bucking forward and back in the troughs between the small waves but Rosh has lost sight of it and Curl rolls up his trousers and wades for it and throws it again along the beach and Rosh scampers after it barking. And as he comes out of the water Curl sees Melior standing there, further up the beach, his rucksack as usual over his shoulder but it hangs loose and looks empty.

Curl walks slowly towards him feeling uncertain because they haven't exchanged more than a few words since the disaster with Cecelia, but as he gets close enough to speak Melior says, 'How are you old boy?' and as they turn to walk together along the sand he puts a reassuring arm around Curl's shoulders.

Nathan Stockman was sure Dawn Clegg could get away so long as she had a passport and Melior said she had – she'd shown it to him, it dated from some years back but it was still valid. It was the problem of getting her booked on a ship he thought would hold them up but Nathan said no. Now he and Felice had made up their minds to go he didn't feel like wasting any time and he'd watched the shipping news and visited shipping agents. He and Felice had a booking already – a two-berth cabin for next month. But if they'd been willing to take bunks in six-berth cabins they could have got away sooner. It was true there were

93

forty or more ships in port, half of them anchored out in the stream, but the passenger ships were getting away because there weren't the same problems with loading . . .

Felice lay back among cushions on the big bed that seemed almost to fill the room, while Nathan and Pat and Melior and Curl sat in a tight half-circle on deck-chairs in the space that remained. Curl's chair faced almost directly towards the bed, and while the talk went on between Nathan and Melior he took in the firm pale flesh of Felice who was turning over pages of a musical score, humming sometimes, occasionally releasing a note which raced to all corners like a flock of birds beating to get out. Now and then she looked up from the score to offer a comment about shipping and about their own plans, hers and Nathan's, and when she saw Curl looking at her appreciatively she smiled back at him in that way she had which was so direct and frank and lacking in concealment he took it always to be motherly or big-sisterly so his ardour was checked and he felt put in his place . . .

There was the problem of money, Melior was saying – and here he felt really stumped. He usually had a bit to come and go on but since this wharf business he'd been contributing all he could to the strike fund as well as a little bit of extra to an old friend so there was just nothing he could draw on. If it hadn't been for the garden he would hardly have been able to feed himself and Cecil decently, and he just didn't have any new work ready that he could offer for sale. But Nathan said that needn't be an obstacle either. The money-tree had bloomed for him, the Insurance had said they would pay out on his house, and although it wasn't a lot it left him a small surplus. He'd been going to make a long-term-no-interest-forget-it-if-you-have-to loan to Curl and Pat to get them through the year but if they could make do with a bit less there would be enough to cover a fare to get Dawn Clegg to England or to Spain.

And Pat who hadn't felt quite easy about the loan said they could certainly get by with less; and Curl who didn't think they could and who regretted having to give any of it up, agreed with her and allowed himself, as a reward, a long luxurious look at the tight cleft that was showing where the buttons of Felice's dress were open, and as if in response Felice sang a full note, directing it at him like an arrow, smiling and half-closing her eyes.

'So that's that,' Melior concluded as the room was cleared of Felice's reverberations. 'We just have to organize the details and keep her out of sight. And for Christ's sake let's all keep quiet about it. If she goes back in there it's a life sentence. She really will go mad. And believe me – Cecil's as sensitive and as eccentric as they come but I've never met anyone saner.'

And from his hospital bed Mr Roy Belsham whom the Prime Minister has described as maimed and whom the hospital describes as recovering from slight concussion and abrasions inflicted by a blow on the head with a plaster dog, broadcasts to the nation urging old unionists to join the new obliging unions, of which he is the President, and everyone to support the Government in its tireless efforts to bring about industrial harmony at home, and abroad the defeat of the Red tide.

So a few days pass, a week, and the comic strip goes on, and as the night sky closes over, Patagonia walks at the water's edge thinking of Jim and June gone out there through the gateway to the world, and Nathan and Felice going, and now Cecelia Skyways – listening to the small waves break and counting the lights that flash and wink across the Gulf from the shores of Rangitoto, and makes out in the darkness the pale phallic tower of the lighthouse directly across, and yearns beyond the freshness of the breeze on her face towards the infinity of the night. She has tried to be de Thierry, she has tried to be Aorewa, but she feels neither French nor Maori nor Celt nor even plain Pat Bennett but she is perhaps the vast desert emptiness of Patagonia through which she imagines the winds of the southern world ceaselessly howling. What is it all about, she wonders, feeling that life is vast beyond management or comprehension and that love is the same; and when she thinks of Curl she feels at this moment nothing and her eyes fill with tears at the emptiness of it. If he were smaller, she thinks, if she could hold him like a baby – it is a thought that has come to her lately – and in a moment all her wishing has contracted to that image of the small shape in her arms, the soft fluffy head, the milky smell of its breath, one small beautiful living receptacle for the French blood, the Maori, the English and the Celt, like rivers converging and merging with the German and the English and whatever else there are in Urlich's veins, a child she would call Siegfried or Sieglinde, who would know what the waves are saying and what comes on the wind and what is flashed from the beacon and what the island feels sunk in its stone composure, who would walk this beach and read all the languages that to its mother are puzzling and obscure. So as the shadow of Curl Skidmore comes over the sand, hesitating because he's nervous, not knowing how he will be received, she flings herself at him, taking him in a headlock and throwing him to the sand where they wrestle and roll about and it is a while before he knows whether this assault is friendly or savage, the two are so close.

And up on her verandah at that very moment Mrs Battle is pleased but hiding her pleasure because it isn't good for the boy, inspecting her son Charles who is dressed in his ticket-clipping uniform, the only uniform he has, shoe polish, button polish, belt polish, hat-badge polish, hat straight, tie straight, buttons done up, trousers creased – and back straight, Charles, shoulders back please, head up, that's it, toes at ten-to-two – and gives him a grudging pass hiding her satisfaction which wouldn't be good for him, might make him slack on it – and off he goes, marching up the drive to do his duty, to join the Civil Emergency Organization, to keep the Reds at bay, to drive them out from under the bed. Mrs Battle is with you, Prime Minister, and so is Charles, and there are many thousands of Mrs Battle and many thousands of Charles.

And, 'The Government must act rather than talk,' writes the *Star* leader writer, who is determined to meet the Challenge, and especially the Challenge of his rival on the bad chair in the *Herald* office down the road. 'The Government should announce that crowds on the waterfront will be dispersed without hesitation, and that The Police Will Be Armed. And the Government should make it known that should individuals or groups defy the ban and challenge the authority of the police, The Police will Shoot.'

And, 'Bang Bang,' says Charles Battle to himself, marching through the streets on his way to join the new Civil Emergency Organization.

So now see if you can see it as it appears to Kenneth Blayburn as he's named in the records or to little Kenny as he's known on the wharf and on the seats outside the ferry building after midnight, see if you can see it as it appears to him in the morning coming in too late to join his mates outside the wharf gates so he is behind the line of police who have linked arms and are driving the union men down the street making room for the new obliging unionists who will soon be arriving. And Ken is too short to see over the heads of the police, to see what's happening on the other side of that line of black helmets and broad shoulders and uniform jackets drawn up and rumpled as the linked arms drag or push forward and the shiny heels lift off the ground and the toes drive down and there is a groaning heaving sound as of a rugby scrum. But he can see the felt hats on the tallest of the unionists and they are pointing away, they are not facing the police and the batons haven't been drawn so they are allowing themselves to be pushed away down the street and for a moment it looks as though Ken might be left on the right side of the law and at that he becomes Charlie Chaplin or his old self and with an almighty run he scampers lightly up and over the backs of the heaving policescrum and lands in the midst of his mates on the other side. For a few seconds he is carried this way and that, his feet not reaching the ground, and then as the men open a gap for him he sinks into it and sees nothing but the shirts and shoulders and arms and trousers around him and the sky and the cranes and buildings above. The whole crowd of unionists is making itself as inert and heavy as it can. But now the momentum is stepped up, Ken feels himself moving faster, the policescrum is making a rush and the

97

unionists are being driven up into Queen Street and with the speed of the rush the crowd is breaking up and Ken finds himself washed up on the granite steps of the Post Office. And now as the mass of men is scattered he can see the whole scene for the first time – the army with rifles and walkie-talkie radios standing just inside the wrought iron wharf-gates and the black police patrol cars and the police line that has driven them into Queen Street drawing back nearer to the gates, while the first of the army lorries are beginning to move towards the gates, making their way through the crowds of police and soldiers. The shout goes up among the union men who are re-forming that those trucks are bringing in the scabs, the scabs are in the trucks, and there is a rush towards the gates where the police haven't yet re-formed. Ken finds himself running with the others, they have got up some speed, the police are turning to face them, trying to link arms, to re-form their lines, but the unionists are breaking through and the trucks are held up and Ken is tearing at the fabric on the sides of the trucks while others are opening doors and shouting at drivers to stop, to get out, to go into reverse. Everyone is shouting, whistles are blasting, orders are yelled, radios are crackling, rifles are being banged about, boots are stamping this way and that, some trucks are stalled and are being rocked, someone is shouting they should be set on fire, and at the backs of the trucks the new unionists are showing faces briefly and withdrawing under a hail of abuse and rotten fruit. Now there is a line of khaki as well as a line of black and Ken doesn't know which way he is going, he is crushed and feels as if his body is being driven in two directions, one at right angles to the other, and then all at once a space clears and he sees what looks like a familiar face, the uniform he thinks of as 'ours', the rifle he knows so well how to handle, and it seems to happen in slow motion, the way it rises in the gap, backed by a grimacing, long-jawed face, and he has time to think, This has happened before, as the butt comes cracking down and he sinks to his knees, the blood running into his eye.

It must be about this time, a little before, a little after, that U. A. Skidmore, third-year Arts Faculty student at Auckland

University College is sitting in Somervell's coffee shop writing a poem which he will dedicate to P. de T. A. Bennett, second-year student in the Elam School of Fine Arts, a poem which arises from but is not in any direct or obvious way about, her attack on him at the water's edge last evening and what followed on the sand and against the retaining wall and in the grass under the pohutukawas and on the floor of the verandah flat and in the bed and on through the night. He is still dazed by it but his mind clears itself of confusion as the images are marshalled, the dominant one (he doesn't know why) being the island of Rangitoto and beyond it the gap to the open sea that is the gateway to the world. There is a lecture U. A. Skidmore should be attending, there are two lectures, but the hour passes, followed by a second hour, and the poem is written and he sits there, washed out, satisfied, drinking a third cup of coffee which the girl behind the counter has given him free because he has told her he needs it and can't really spare the money. And it's then the shouting and scuffling start up outside and he stuffs his sheets of paper into his jacket pocket and picks up his raincoat from the empty seat beside him and goes out to find himself in the midst of a running battle, or the tail end of it, because the wharfies have been driven up Queen Street all the way from the wharves and the police are scattering the last of them so they won't easily or quickly re-form.

'You blokes get yourselves in trouble,' says the young duty doctor in Casualty at Auckland Public Hospital, 'and then you come to us to patch you up.' And he clips another stitch brutally through Ken Blayburn's forehead and pulls it tight. Ken feels the pain of the stitches and he can see the doctor is unsympathetic but he doesn't know why. He feels sick in the stomach and can't remember how he got a wound to the head. Now the doctor is swabbing the stitches with something that stings and Ken groans.

'Hurts a bit does it?' says the doctor. 'You might think about it next time before you put your head in the way of a truncheon.'

And lying in Mrs Battle's letterbox is a letter airmail from

99

England for Pat and Curl from Jim and June which Mrs Battle herself will bring around to them in the evening and hand up to them through the window as they sit over their meal. She will come step-dragging around the house into the courtyard calling, 'Gurr-l, Gurr-l,' and as she hands up the letter she will tell them that her own Charles has played his part today in the defeat of those evil men. And, 'You must come soon,' the letter says. And, 'Piccadilly Circus . . .' And, 'red pillar boxes . . .' And, 'English spring . . .' And, 'country lanes . . .' And, 'thatched cottages . . .' And, 'castles . . .' And, 'the Channel . . .' And, 'Paris . . .' And, 'Spain . . .'

Melior was hurrying, half-walking, half-trotting, limping to and fro between the studio and the hut where Dawn Clegg, alias Cecelia Skyways, was lying so sick she thought she might as well die. 'Surely the diseases themselves wouldn't be any worse,' she said faintly, because she was only ill with the inoculations she had had in preparation for her departure abroad. 'I've never felt so ill in my whole life, Melior. I just want to die.'

'Ah but you won't,' he said. 'Soon you'll be better and then you'll be off on your travels.'

She smiled wanly as he mopped her brow. 'I can't imagine it,' she said.

'Just keep sipping the water,' he said, 'so you don't get dehydrated. Your temperature's still high. I'll leave the lantern on for now. I'll be back later to see how you're doing.'

Outside it was dark. As he approached his back door he saw what looked like a sack of potatoes, but it was too large for that, and it was wearing a hat. It had slumped on his step. There were some stitches in its forehead and blood all down its face and it smelled abominably of vomit.

'Something's happened Mel,' it said. 'I'm not sure . . .' And then it keeled over.

'Thank God he's small,' Melior thought, as he dragged it indoors.

SEVEN

Exit and Enter

The long armies of the rain come always unarmed.

When I went down to the water I took with me
my head my heart and my hands
my head in my hands and my hand on my heart.
I took my heart and all its dreams.

Singing in the shower behind the closed curtain
writing on the sheets and writhing under them
walking letter by letter across the white plain
whispering on the roof as the armies go over
sighing on the sand when the waves retreat
filling with her full body
        the form of the form of the poem –

Never to let the letters
        never to fullstop the starts
is why she weeps and pleads.

Let her tell your misfortune.
Let her tell you how the dream ends.

So now I address you directly Curl Skidmore, Urlich Ambrose.
Who else has the right? Melior, your dear old mentor, has gone
to his long comic strip home where he has put gold harps into
the hands of feather-winged angels and speech balloons into
their goldfish mouths. The momma and the father have long
since swallowed the father's defeat in Mt Eden South. They
have become two large white eternal clouds edged with pink
appearing from time to time, always surprised to find
themselves there, sailing beyond the Gulf over the gateway to

the world. And Patagonia – where is she? You've heard of course that she made a name for herself (the name was Aorewa de Thierry) as a mural painter and stage designer in London, and that she went from there to a big job in Munich, and from Munich to Stockholm, and from Stockholm . . . And that there was a marriage, and another marriage, and something that was not a marriage but better . . . Word always gets back. There are the blue aerogrammes, and the cards at Christmas, and the gossip of the migratory godwits which are our souls in flight between the two hemispheres and our hearts' two homes. No aerogramme has gone from her to you direct, no card, no exact transcription of godwit gossip. But indirectly you have heard. It is a roundabout way of saying the harsh truth – that she too might as well be dead. And Jim and June came back and went farming north of Kaitaia. And Nathan and Felice climbed their ladders, together, and then separately, and can still be heard up there, out there, on the radio waves, in the beams of the sky. And Mrs Battle step-dragged once and forever into the shadows and Clipper Charles retired and was awarded a pair of silver snips. And Cecelia Skyways published her *Memoirs of a Railway Siding* and became a household word. So I address you directly, Curl Skidmore, Urlich Ambrose – who else is here to do it? 'Let her tell you how the dream ends,' you wrote – fine words! – and then you packed away your paper and your typewriter and took out your French prose for the week and worked at it through the squally morning. Across the yard there had been recently that same movement in the flat that had belonged to Jim and June – the bobbing up and down as Nathan and Felice jumped inside their tea-chests to pack down all the things they couldn't bear to part with and which sea travel made it possible to take. And the same to-ing and fro-ing – out to the passport office, to the bank, to the travel agent, to the doctor. All of it so closely followed those pre-departure activities of Jim and June and now you could pick by the increasing momentum that the day was getting closer. Already it had arrived for Cecelia Skyways. You had said goodbye to her last night, her luggage was loaded on board ship and today Melior would be taking her over on the ferry and seeing her safely on board, and

Pat would be coming down from Art School and Melior and Pat would be waving from the wharf. You would have gone too but Cecelia wanted someone to wave from the beach in front of Mrs Battle's house. Jim and June had said in one of their letters that they had seen the house quite clearly from the ship as it sailed down the Gulf inside Rangitoto. And it was obvious Cecelia hoped the person who stayed behind would be you, Curl Skidmore, and you had said you would – you would wave a red towel. And you had held her two pale hands and kissed her freckled cheek and she had shyly kissed yours and nothing had been said about the hour you had spent together in the hut but it was understood (wasn't it?) that you were sorry, that you knew you had made a botch of it, and that she bore you no grudge. The red towel would wave from the empty beach and Cecelia at the rail would see it and that would be a Sign, from you to her, a seal upon your affection for one another. You had the towel ready, Pat had put it out for you, and you had done your morning exercise in verse and now you had your French dictionary out and you were allowing yourself a moment to listen to the news and to make a cup of coffee and a peanut butter sandwich before settling to your prose. It all seemed systematic and orderly, didn't it Early Ambrose, as it was meant to, but the news recounted how the wharf unionists had been routed again and the new unions were slowly forming at the separate ports to replace the national union that had been deregistered and how meanwhile the uniformed services were magnificently holding the line, and that news, though it was more or less the same you had heard every day for three months, angered you and upset your feeling of purpose so you had to have a second cup of coffee and a second peanut butter sandwich before work on the dreary French prose could go on. And while you ate the sandwich and drank the coffee standing at the sink in the little kitchen you looked across the yard as you had done from time to time during the morning. There hadn't been much action over there but now Nathan came out dressed for town, his brown shoes polished, his corduroys pressed, his woven tie neatly knotted, a red silk scarf just visible inside the collar of his long gabardine coat, his tweed hat at a slight but not rakish angle, and his thin briefcase tucked under one arm. He looked across to you, hesitating for a moment in the doorway, turning up his collar against the rain, and then with a wave of the hand he headed up the drive. Behind him the windows of the little flat stared blindly at you, Ambrosia. There was no movement behind them, no carolling Felicevoice, and you tried not to think of her there, warm and white and inviting in the big bed.

And in the hut in Melior Farbro's back garden Cecelia stood looking for the last time at the matting on the floor and on the walls and at the neat stretcher bed and at the one web she had left over the door and at the one spider, still and watchful, at its centre. 'Melior's promised to leave you there,' she told Bodhidharma of the Web, 'and he says little Ken won't touch you, so you're safe for your old age, my friend. I'm grateful for your advice and it wasn't your fault I was a bad pupil. In any case I'll be working on myself, you can be sure of that. You did a better job than the Department of Electricity, that's why I'm running away from them. You know I'm not running away from you. I'll need another master in Spain and that shouldn't be difficult but I'm sure I won't find a better one. I'm sorry this sort of farewell distresses you – you regard it as sentimental Westernism I suppose and I suppose it is but as you said to me just the other day in the very voice of my own dear mother, I believe in giving credit where it's due. I haven't forgotten that Monkey pissed between the fingers of the Buddha and neither should you, Body, so keep your tongue in your cheek if you start giving advice to little Ken, won't you boy. His head seems worse than mine was when I came here. Poor Melior, he wants to be an artist but he seems to have some sort of head hospital instead of a studio. But that's Melior calling and Oh my word doesn't he sound agitated the poor old sausage . . .'

And suddenly she did a little skip, jamming a strange blue velvet hat over her ginger-gold aureole of hair. 'Do you realize where I'm going today, Body? I'm going to *Spain*!'

An artist's studio, thought U. A. Skidmore, third-year Arts

Faculty student at the Auckland University College who was doing his weekly French prose at the window of the verandah flat that looked out over the Gulf towards Rangitoto. That's an 'atelier' – but is it masculine or feminine? And he paused for a moment, thinking, not of Melior's studio which was not a mile away, but of the pictures of Cézanne's atelier he'd seen in one of the books Pat had brought home from Art School. It had a cast-iron stove, and beautiful blue painted screens, and from the windows you could see an overgrown garden, and beyond the poplar trees in the garden there was a view across fields to the town of Aix-en-Provence. And in other pictures of the town of Aix-en-Provence there were little cobbled streets and a market square with a fountain and a café with tables out of doors where Cézanne had sat brooding over the reception of his paintings in Paris . . .

And U. A. Skidmore, third-year student, woke from this particular reverie to find himself once again in the kitchen unscrewing the lid of the peanut butter jar and staring across the yard to where the windows of the little flat that had been Jim and June's, and now was Nathan and Felice's, and soon would be nobody's, until the next couple came and went to London and Paris and Aix-en-Provence and Madrid, stared blindly out at the rain that seemed to be easing. Did he imagine he would find whether 'atelier' was masculine or feminine by opening the peanut butter jar? – and he screwed the lid shut again. But he saw beside it on the sink bench the shopping list Pat had made for him. He'd forgotten he was to do the shopping this morning, and it had to be done in time for him to be in position on the beach with the red towel as Cecelia's ship sailed out. In other words, the sooner the better. So he went into the bedroom and brushed his hair and chose a tie and knotted it and took out a jacket and looked for money and in general prepared himself for shopping at Takapuna while his mind drifted back to those images of Cézanne's studio and the town of Aix-en-Provence where it was difficult to imagine anyone (except Cézanne himself of course) could be unhappy.

The taxi that was to take them and Cecil's last suitcase to the ferry wharf at Northcote was at the gate and of course Melior was fussing and he knew he was fussing but knowing made no difference. It was hard to get Cecil to move or to have any sense of time, and since she had been reading those Buddhist books it had got worse. And now there was Kenny, little Ken, sitting all day with a heavy frown trying to remember what had happened. He was beautifully clean and Melior had enjoyed washing him from head to foot and dressing his wound and looking after him, but now there was this awful sluggishness that was so unlike Ken, and his anxiety that even though he'd been told what happened and what it was all about he couldn't remember. Why should it matter? – but it did, so there he sat all day, frowning, not the lively little Charlie Chaplin figure Melior had dreamed so long would come back and light up his life. So it was good Cecil was going though he would miss her terribly, she was a darling, and Melior felt for a moment stricken at the thought of it but then the taxi tooted again and he called angrily, 'Skyways, Dawn god damn you – are you going to Spain or am I?' – and there she was on the path, carrying her suitcase and smiling under an absurd and charming hat of blue velvet.

And now we are watching you Curl Skidmore, coming down the steps into the little white courtyard. The rain has cleared for the moment and you are chancing it without a coat and instead of taking the most direct line to the path that climbs the ridge behind the house and leads to the road and the shops you do a sort of half circle, skirting the edge of the yard so you go nearer than necessary to the windows of the little outhouse flat – and there she is in bed, Felice, and she hears your step and looks back over the bed-head to see you and she calls, 'Hullo Curlyboy,' and reaches up to push the window open so you can exchange a word and as she does the cover falls from one of her breasts and there it is, large and ripe with a big red nipple, and she doesn't do anything about covering it but yawns and stretches so its twin is uncovered. 'Oh has it stopped raining at last,' she says, stretching and twisting over on to her stomach so she is facing you out in the yard. And because the floor-level of the outhouse flat is only an inch or two higher than ground level in the yard, you are looking in at her and she is looking out at you as if you are both in the same room, with only the partition of the wall below the window between. 'Where are you going to my pretty boy?' sings Felice, and you say you are going to do the shopping and she tells you to bring yourself nearer, to lean in the window, because she wants to look at your tie which she thinks is beautiful. You lean in the window and she looks at your tie and she strokes it and admires it and says it's lovely and moves this way and that shedding blankets and uncovering a beautiful belly and a surprising bush, a flowering shrub of pubic hair. We are watching you Curl Skidmore and we can see even across the vast gulf of thirty and more years that you are lost in a reverie more powerful even than the atelier of Cézanne and the cafés of Aix-en-Provence, and if any thoughts go along with it they are taking a form such as, 'I'm not going to make the same mistake twice.' But in any case we can see that no such thought is needed, Felice will not let you make any mistakes, already your fingers are running over those big red-nipples and down into the flowering shrub, and if Mrs Battle should round the corner now she would see a strange sight – her young tenant, Curl Skidmore, disappearing head-first through the window of the outhouse flat as if sucked inside by an enormous vacuum cleaner.

So now we see the taxi taking Melior Farbro and the duly passported Dawn Clegg down to the ferry wharf at Northcote and Melior stretches his back and relaxes beside her knowing that they are in time to catch the ferry which in turn will get them across to the town side in time to get Cecil and her last suitcase around to the ship before it departs. And it must be while this is going on and while Melior is paying the driver and the driver is taking Cecil's suitcase from the boot that Felice is unwrapping Curl Skidmore like a Christmas parcel dragging at garments and throwing them this way and that with little squeals as more and more is revealed until there it is, and Felice looks at it and looks at Curl and looks at it again and says, 'I love cocks better than . . . better than *oysters*!' And she bends over

107

to nuzzle it and close her lips around the base of it. Felice doesn't believe in rushing her pleasures, so probably Melior Farbro and the passported Dawn are already aboard the ferry, scenting the salt smell around the wooden piles and seeing the green water under Northcote wharf as ropes are cast off and engines begin to go full ahead out across the harbour towards the taller skyline when Curl looks down and catches the extraordinary perspective of his balls on either side of the Felicechin and her lips between them and his erect cock by-passing her nose, obliterating one eye and passing on up over her forehead bisecting transversely the line of her hair. And while Felice is taking her time there, pleasing herself and him too but not so as to advance things too rapidly, Curl's hands are everywhere, it is a long and luxurious exploration, so the ferry could well have crossed most of the harbour among the ships anchored in the stream, it could even be pulling into the city ferry wharf under the clock tower and not far from Princes Wharf where Dawn Clegg's ship is waiting to take her to Spain, before the positions on the big bed have radically changed and it is Felice of course who has determined the change. Now if Mrs Battle should step-drag into the yard and look across to the outhouse flat she would see nothing more surprising than a drawn curtain and though it would be possible for her to twitch aside the curtain from out in the yard it is improbable she would do such a thing and just as well since she has once already suffered some kind of intracranial vascular accident causing her leg to drag and her speech to slur. But we are watching you, Urlich Ambrose, and we don't think you will object after thirty and more years if we report that your eyes are round as saucers and your mouth clamped over what in the first year of the second half of the twentieth century was called in bars and army barracks and freezing works and metal foundries but never in print a cunt, and that your arms are reaching up at the same time, the thumb and forefinger of each hand pulling at a large red nipple, and that while your mouth is at its work you are seeing with those saucer-round eyes up over the rounded white landscape to where your hands are at work and beyond to where the rolling Feliceface sighs and looks down at what you are doing and closes its eyes and opens them and looks again, so you have a curious feeling, lying flat on your stomach with your mouth securely clamped, breathing through your nose which is fixed in the flowering bush, and with your hands stretched ahead of you accomplishing their nipplework, that you are engaged in some kind of swimming exercise, and then again, or at the same time, that the Felicebody is a large white rubber balloon you are inflating and that you and it are floating out on some hitherto unimaginable sea, a pleasurecruise to end them all. Time must necessarily in this report be inexact but it is certainly possible that Melior and Dawn Clegg and Dawn Clegg's last suitcase have already reached Princes Wharf and have been checked through to proceed on board before the first orthodox entry is achieved on the big bed and it is an entry seeming to you so dreamlike so smooth . . . There's nothing premature about the first ejaculation but it isn't long delayed either. So you, Curlyboy, roll on your back staring and smiling at something a trick of momentary light on water in the yard has painted on the ceiling, some voluptuary vision, and close your eyes and sleep, watched over by the basking Felice who knows a little sleep will do wonders. Now there is time to see Dawn Clegg to her cabin, a six-berther close to the water which she is to share with a set of her young countrywomen she will call 'the hearty party' who look like mountain climbers and speak with those curved and badgered vowels which signify in 1951 private schools, virginity, and a recent presentation at Government House. All is excitement and mad laughter in the cabin and in the lounges and Melior is looking everywhere for Pat who has a boarding pass and is to join him saying goodbye to Cecil but when the 'All Visitors Ashore' is called she still hasn't arrived. Now there are tears in Melior's eyes and tears in Cecil's but they are smiling too and she promises to keep up her *Memoirs of a Railway Siding* and to keep out of trouble and to let him know if she needs money urgently and to send him a wineskin and to write, and he in turn promises to write and to send her copies of anything Curl publishes and to find some money for her any time she really needs it and to keep up the series she hasn't been allowed to see and maybe to send her photographs of some of them when they're put on show. 'Goodbye Cecil.' 'Goodbye Melior,' – unbelievable words! – and he is off down the gangway, still looking out for Pat, and Cecelia is taking her place at the rail when Curl wakes feeling he is no longer a swimmer he is horse, because Felice hasn't waited for him to wake, she has gone to work with resuscitative hand and mouth (the kiss of life) on the piece of him that matters most and it has jumped half out of bed while he remained sleeping on his back and Felice is astride it on her knees, riding it up and down inside her faster and faster, tossing her head and whinnying as if she were horse as well as rider, and now Curl is joining the action, they are taking fences together, he is bucking against her, she is settling closer over him and tightening on him, locking herself there with elbows and knees like a little white jockey and 'Oh,' she says, head thrown back, using that word which in the first year of the second half of the twentieth century is sometimes used in bedrooms but never in print, 'I'm just a cunt,' and that must be about the moment when Melior, who has given up all hope of Pat, feels a hand on his arm and she is there, breathless. 'I couldn't find the right wharf,' Pat says, 'and half of them are surrounded by the army. But look Melior, I've got some streamers.' Pat remembers what happened when Jim and June were leaving, how the crane pulled down all the streamers and new ones had to be thrown, so she and Melior don't throw theirs, they wait while others are thrown and sure enough the crane on rails moves and lumbers the full length of the ship gathering the early streamers all over its cabin and boom and the little crowd (it is not a big liner like the one that took Jim and June) sighs and protests and then streamers begin to fly again. This time Pat throws one and Melior throws one and Pat throws another and Dawn Clegg with that blue velvet hat pressed over her electrified head, and with a large knitted muffler now and mittens against the coming rigours of the winter sea, holds a red streamer and a blue streamer and the two lines of coloured paper twist and curve out and shake and sag in the little flurries of rain that are still sailing across from time to time. They wave and smile to one another back and forth from ship to shore and wait for the tugs to get into position and for the last hatches and iron doors to be clamped shut. And while they wait there is the sound of shouting and booing further along Quay Street where a shift of the new obliging union is being ferried through a picket line in army lorries. And while they wait Mrs Battle is listening to an interview with Minister of Labour Sullivan who is congratulating himself on not giving in to terrortactics, and Charles is quietly and precisely clipping, keeping himself in reserve for what he may be called upon to do as a member of the Civil Emergency Organization, and Ken is sitting alone in Melior's house frowning and thinking, 'And then I stuffed the trousers into the culvert because of the paint . . .', and the Prime Minister on a visit to Auckland is saying to his private secretary that he has met an English immigrant called McMullin, an ex-guardsman and an excellent chap, who would make a better President of the new obliging Cargoworkers' Union than that Belsham who got skittled with the plaster dog. On the big bed in the outhouse flat positions have changed, they have gone back to the old missionary posture, and while they are still engaged in the fuck they are having a sort of conversation or exchange of compliments and jokes and expressions of satisfaction and Felice reaches up and clamps her hands around the back of his neck and says in a minute they're going to take a luxurious bath together and then . . . She means to go on to say that then they will eat a bottle of oysters she has in the kitchen and return to bed but her voice goes into a wobble at a sensation that spreads out in electrical waves engulfing her belly and thighs, drawing them into that centre where the stalwart Skidmore is still stirring. But already the gangplank has gone, the ropes are cast off, the tugs are working, the gap is opening, Dawn Clegg's mittened hand has been waving and the streamers are stretching as the ship moves slowly out from its berth. So Cecelia is probably clear of the wharf, still able to pick out the heads of Melior and Pat in the crowd but seeing them diminishing, when Felice stands at the door of the outhouse flat with a towel around her, Curl beside her also with towel, and Felice inches the door open and looks out. The yard is empty, the coast clear as she opens the door wide and pushes him out like a parachute instructor pushing out a flying cadet making his first jump. Curl makes a dash across the corner of the courtyard to the outhouse bathroom and in a moment Felice has followed. If this strange exit and entrance is seen by Rosh who is passing through on his way to the beach he shows no sign of it but merely lifts his leg in passing at the base of the cabbage tree, scratches a token scratch among the fallen cabbage tree spikes and passes on through the trellis gate across the grass and down on to the sand. The beach is empty but there is a surprising amount of investigative work a dog has to do on an empty beach and it is better done without human distractions so Rosh goes to work at once nosing into a paper bag, while up in the steamfilled bathroom a naked soprano is kissing a naked third-year university student so lovingly and appreciatively it sets his head spinning and his cock climbing again. Now Cecelia's ship, the *Rangitane*, is being turned about into the stream. Cecelia has lost sight of Melior and Pat and is seeing the wharves where a few of the new obliging unionists and some men in khaki are working together, and the buildings of the city, and the brown-orange autumn-into-winter English trees of the Domain sloping up towards the Doric columns of the War Memorial Museum. She can feel under her the throb of the engines as the ship threads its way among the stalled cargo vessels in the harbour towards Devonport and North Head. 'I'm going I'm really going I can't believe it,' thinks Dawn Clegg, terrified and ecstatic all at once, while over the loudspeakers as at the departure of Jim and June come the delicious banalities of 'Anchors Aweigh' and 'Now is the Hour'. Ashore Pat and Melior have turned away with that feeling of emptiness that is so familiar but never diminishes no matter how often you see people leaving, and Pat is saying she will go overseas one of these days, and Melior says no doubt she will, most people who are worth anything in this place do, but thank God some of them come back. They stand at the wharf gates talking about this and that and wondering whether they should go to Somervell's for a cup of coffee to cheer themselves up, but Melior is worrying about little Ken alone in the house with his bad head so in the end they decide against it. Pat has finished at the Art School for the day so they walk back along Quay Street to the ferry building while the *Rangitane* is rounding North Head out of the harbour into the Gulf and in the outhouse flat on Takapuna Beach a beautifully bathed and scented soprano wearing only a sweater below which her flowering bush stands forth as electrically as hair on Cecelia Skyways' head is forking oysters out of a bottle into the mouth of an equally bathed but not scented third-year student wearing the bathrobe of the soprano's husband, and forking them into her own mouth as well with exclamations of pleasure, alternating the oysters with olives which she takes from another bottle, and with sips of red wine. We watch you, Urlich Ambrose, lunching on oysters and olives and red wine, while your eyes are drawn more and more to the flowering bush, and Felice knows they are and she is pleased with you for it and pleased to keep you waiting because the oysters and olives and wine are so good and because the waiting will make the next and final round in the big bed more delicious when it comes. But watching you Urlich we are worrying because the *Rangitane* has rounded North Head, it is steaming into the Gulf inside Rangitoto, and Cecelia Skyways, known to her passport and to her ticket of passage as Dawn Clegg, is already at the rail checking the coast as it goes by and looking out for her first sign of Takapuna Beach where she knows, or believes she knows, a red towel will be waiting, and it is you, Urlich Ambrose, who have forgotten the towel. Nor do you give a thought, as you swallow another oyster and feel your cock curling out towards the flowering bush, to the possibility that Pat might be already on board a ferry, as indeed she is, sitting in silence beside Melior as they cross towards Northcote. Is it spoiling the beauty of your sport in the outhouse flat to say that even as you slide a hand under the sweater to remind yourself of the full tight beauty of the globes Felice wears there the electrified head of Cecelia Skyways is straining forwards, checking this tree and that headland and the other house to be sure that the long empty stretch of sand with houses rising behind it which she can now see clearly from the rail is in fact Takapuna, and that the white house with the white outhouses is in fact Mrs Battle's, that she has made no mistake, and yet still there is no red towel, nowhere a sign of one because you,

Ambrosia, are backing Felice to the bed, you are kissing her, you are going down on your knees while she stands dragging the sweater over her head and uncovering her bobbing breasts and looking at them in the mirror and at you on your knees burying your forgetful ecstatic face in the flowering bush and in the beautiful swamp at its base. Would you now if your mind could for a moment admit the vision of a puzzled golden head under a blue velvet hat checking and rechecking the landmarks and staring unbelieving at a white house with not so much as a dot of red in front – would you be able to disengage, to rush forth and do your towelish duty? Of course you would not, and perhaps it's as well that in a comic strip world where so much is ghastly and so much more is less than the heart desires, there should be, even if only for a short space, a capsule within which the illusion (or perhaps it is not an illusion) of perfection has been attained. So we will not press upon you at this moment the vision of a disappointed angel at the rail of a receding ship but will permit you untroubled the long slow deliberate slide of your re-entry, acknowledging in the terms of the Zen Master of Cecelia Skyways, Bodhidharma of the Web, that here there is no before and no after, and that here, at one with one another, with Great Creating Nature, and with the Universe, you are in a state of satori and of Grace.

Melior Farbro gets down from the bus, waves to Pat as it pulls away, and hurries down the road to his gate. He doesn't like to hurry in the street because it makes his limp more obvious, and he does a little skip now and then which brings his two legs into line again as they get gradually out of phase. He is stopped by the lady across the street who wants him to sign a petition to the local council about having dogs kept on leashes so they won't foul 'other people's properties'. She has photographic evidence to support her case. 'Oh no,' Melior says, edging around her and backing towards his gate. He doesn't think dogs should be tied up all the time. 'Too noisy. Yapping little brutes.'

'But you can have their barks removed these days,' she says, following him with her paper on its clipboard.

'Removed!' Melior exclaims, edging through the gate and pushing it shut. She has her eye fixed on him but she runs into the obstruction of the shut gate.

'Terrible weather,' Melior says, and he does a skip to adjust his feet on the narrow path and hurries indoors. Little Ken is down on the floor in his underpants. His trousers are rolled into a ball and he is stuffing them into an empty space at the bottom of the bookcase. Melior stares at him, wondering. Ken looks up.

'Sorry,' he says, still on all fours. 'I was just going through it in my mind. I stuffed the trousers in the culvert because of the paint. It was Fred threw the plaster dog. Roy's old lady threw it at us and Fred – he's a real big joker – threw it back and it donged Roy. I thought the trousers . . .'

'You'd better put them back on old boy,' Melior says, 'and get up off the floor. I'll put the kettle on. How's the head feeling now? Any better?'

And about this time, or perhaps five or ten minutes later, Pat Bennett is drifting about the verandah flat trying to read the signs. The big red towel is lying folded exactly where she left it on the yellow table in front of the three-speed tablegram the momma gave Curl for his twenty-first and beside the lamp that has a Japanese design on its shade. Is it possible he could have waved the towel from the beach and returned it, perfectly folded, to the exact same spot? She has a sinking feeling that he has forgotten to wave. But how could he forget? She goes to the window and looks towards the sea. There is no sign of the ship. Or rather, there is a white disappearing dot catching momentary light away out on the furthest horizon beyond Rangitoto that might be it. Cecelia is gone. Pat looks down at the table and sees his French prose which he planned to finish in the morning. There is only half a sentence, which stops at the word 'atelier'. She goes to the kitchen and looks in the cupboards. The shopping list she left him is gone from the sink bench but none of the items on it are in the cupboards or the safe. She begins to feel anxious. An accident . . . She looks across to the outhouse flat. A curtain is drawn over the window of the bed-sitting-room but she can see the window is open. They must be home or the window would be shut . . .

Felice's last trick is the entry from behind. She likes to save it for last and combine as many pleasures as possible, and watching too, as she does now, resting forward on left elbow and top of head, looking up between to see her breasts hanging there, her own fingers moving in circles through the flowering bush and the Curlcock splendidly entering from behind. And there is a gathering momentum, the Curlcock's entries meeting the three fingers circling in their Girl Guide salute, faster and faster. And it has to be remembered that Felice is a singer so it's not any wish to announce by sheer volume that she is in the big-time-sex-league that calls forth these cries and gurgles and warbles and gasps, it's just the readiest mode, the most natural to her, by which to give vent to what is now gathering, is already rolling from the four quarters of her encompassing being, and for a moment you, Urlich Ambrose, catch sight in side view of this magnificence in the mirror, so you are yourself and outside yourself, the human extremity, the great moment which is like the moment of ultimate pain, of death perhaps, when the soul that lives in the mirror sees itself die, when the light watches itself flare and fade, and then you too went down under the waves of it and came up slowly, panting and smiling, to see two still brown eyes in a beautiful olive-skinned face watching you from the window.

What was it you felt, what was it you thought, at that moment, Patagonia? Urlich Skidmore throws the question into the dark night of the 1980s and hears back in the voice he remembers and would recognize anywhere even after a gap of so many decades, I felt nothing, I wanted to die, I thought what a good fuck, I felt hate, I felt love, I felt cold, I felt hot, I thought why haven't *we* done that, I thought what a big cock he's got, I thought so that's why he didn't wave the towel, I thought is it too late to do the shopping, I felt jealousy, I felt indifference, I felt embarrassment, I felt disgust, I felt tired of feeling, I thought Felice's bum is beautiful, I thought I will paint them, I thought it will be better than my seawall picture, and what I thought and felt I don't remember and if I did I wouldn't tell you so it's your business now Mr Whatsit (I've forgotten your name) since it's you who is writing this book and haven't you got an imagination that will fill in the gaps?

Dawn Clegg is still at the rail. The coast, a far distant blurr of cloud with momentary patches of green, is still just visible out there. The sea has turned a deep dark blue out of which washes, as the waves break, a paler blue and a pure white. For the first time Dawn Clegg knows what 'navy blue' means. She is still wearing her mittens and her muffler and her velvet hat, and now the winds are making themselves felt and the ship is rolling and pitching, she is glad of them. She is still thinking about the red towel. She is sure she looked at the right beach. She checked so many landmarks, and checked them so often, but since they are no longer there to be checked again, she has begun to doubt. Yet it seems unreasonable to doubt, and she has been through a dozen scenarios that might explain why Early was late, or why he wasn't there at all, none of them involving sopranos, oysters, olives, red wine or hot baths. What she comes back to is that whatever the reason for his not having appeared with the towel he's not the sort of person you should count on . . . But then Dawn Clegg thinks of Pat and all at once her heart hardens. Pat was late arriving at the wharf. She didn't come on board so there wasn't a chance to talk to her. What had she been doing? Where did she come from? Did she leave Curl somewhere that made it impossible for him to get to the beach in time? What a weakling he is to allow himself to be so manipulated, so controlled, so possessed. It is Pat, possessive Pat, who has made everything go wrong. One day she will write a story about it – and as the gong sounds over the loud speakers and darkness gathers over the waters, Cecelia Skyways, author of *Memoirs of a Railway Siding*, smiles a small smile and turns her mind to the prospect of Spain.

They haven't eaten much, there isn't much to eat because he forgot to do the shopping and now the shops are shut. He is still

117

trying to do his French prose, he has got into the sentence after the one containing the atelier, but he's stuck and hasn't the strength to get unstuck. Pat is dabbing at her practical work and she won't talk about what happened with Felice. When he gets up the courage and the strength to mention it, to approach it obliquely (which is all he can manage) she shakes her head, she doesn't want to talk about it, there's just nothing to be said. The peanut butter jar is empty, the bread is finished, a spring tide is beating itself silly against the sea wall, and he thinks of Cecelia out there, unwaved at, unredtowelled, and wonders will she be seasick, will she be angry, will she be sad? He thinks of his momma who disapproves of him because he has left home to live with a girl he isn't married to, and his sisters who disapprove of him on principle and by habit, and Pat who disapproves of him for a very good and recent reason, and Cecelia who will now disapprove of him because he can't be trusted even to wave a red towel to a black and red ship from a white house on an empty beach. His world is full of disapproving females but there is Felice, warm appreciative oystereating cockgobbling Felice, and he thinks of her with relief and with affection and with a stirring of something else that from now until the Stockmans leave will have to be dealt with severely. And he thinks maybe a walk on the beach . . . But as he gets up to go Pat says very clearly, very audibly, but without turning to look at him, 'Early I'm pregnant. I want you to arrange an abortion.'

EIGHT

And all are False . . .

'Abortion' – it's a word to trigger these days of the eighties talk about rights – the right of the mother to choose, the right to life of the unborn child, the two rights confronting one another on placards and across party lines and down from the pulpit and up from the grass roots. But this was the first year of the second half of the twentieth century and we spoke less about rights and more about laws, and it was the law (for example) that Dawn Clegg alias Cecelia Skyways should go back to the 'convent' and have her head re-electrified because that was what the medical men of the day said should be done with her, and it was the law that if Kenneth Blayburn would not work as many more hours than forty as his employer required he was deemed to be on strike, and it was the law that Patagonia de Thierry Aorewa Bennett must have the child of Urlich Ambrose Skidmore which she had conceived on the night she attacked him with her fierce love-and-wanting in the shallows and on the sand and against the seawall and in the grass under the pohutukawas and on the floor of the verandah flat and in the big bed through the wall from Mrs Battle, while her contraceptive diaphragm lay powdered and boxed in the drawer where she kept her handkerchiefs and scarves. 'Early I'm pregnant. I want you to arrange an abortion.' Factual and practical, but it struck terror to his already unsettled heart and set raging in him a conflict not unlike the one that rages now in public places. He didn't think in terms of rights. It was impossible to think of the mixture of juices inside her, however richly potent, as having rights. And what was the use of Pat having a baby she didn't want? But he was dreadfully, unsettlingly assailed by that manful equivalent of Pat's dreamy imaginings on the beach, the vision of the small furry nodding head, the cuddlesome bundle, and expanding from that the abstract yet somehow quite equally potent thought: he was going to be a *father*. It struck him solemnly, it made him ready for resolutions, for promises of a better life, for self-sacrifice, and with no sense at all that in due course and quite soon humanity – his own – would assert itself again. And mixed in with all this went the fear and the horror – fear of the law, horror at the possibilities, because this was 1951, and abortion figured in the news only when a back-street practitioner was brought to the courts, or when the body of some unfortunate girl for whom the operation had gone disastrously wrong was found dumped under Grafton Bridge or among trees on the lower slopes of the Domain. It was a grave and silent father-to-be (or not to be) that paced the strand and consulted with the night.

But it was no use consulting with the night, with the stars, or even with the lady herself. She wouldn't consider it, she didn't want his child, she wanted to go abroad where everyone else was going, she wanted to get away, and whether this determination had anything to do with what she had seen through the window of the outhouse flat, well he could ask that as often as he liked she simply didn't want to talk about it, she didn't know and it didn't matter. What mattered was that she was too young to be a parent and so was he, they weren't ready for it, they would make a mess of it, it wasn't worth doing unless you really felt you wanted to do it, she'd seen too many snotty-nosed bruised-and-battered kids to want to be the author of one herself and he could drool and swoon and sentimentalize and poeticize all through the verandah flat and along the beach and up and over the hill and across the harbour and back again about how lovely it would be to be a father, it just bloody wouldn't be lovely, he would hate waking in the night and scraping crap off nappies and never being able to go out, he needed about seven pounds extra ballast in his head before he would be ready for that and so would she, and in the meantime she wanted the potent juices removed before they began to solidify into anything she could even vaguely think of as a child. It was her fault they were there she knew that and she took full blame for the mad crazy idea that had run away with her but she was going to take the backstreet risk, he must make the arrangement. And for all Curl's asking did it mean and would they after and were they going to, plain Pat Bennett was taking it practically, step by step, and what it meant and would they after and were they going to could be thought about and decided on later when the abortion had been accomplished. Her laugh when he offered to marry her just as soon as she liked wasn't even unkind. She patted both his cheeks at once and kissed his forehead and told him that for an intelligent boy he showed a remarkable capacity for omelette thinking and he went away not understanding why she'd laughed, not understanding even what she meant by omelette thinking unless it had something maybe to do with scrambling everything together. But at least she'd kissed him and that anyway was something.

But that kiss, Earlyboy, you should have known it was goodbye – not that she was heading that very moment for the door, but wasn't there an indulgence in it that signified the end of the dream in which the four of you, Curl and Pat and Jim and June, had walked back along the beach from Nathan Stockman's restaurant, two steps forward and one step back, and you had wound off the spare spools in your head your endless seeming remembering of poems by double-dyed Dylan and the unmanly Hopkins while the still summernight sky blew blessing upon you, and you were her mystery-man and her brilliant-future man and her lover-man and all the rest of it? It was not so long ago but what had happened to all that magic, and to the two novels that went with it, wound up and waiting to be delivered, and to the determination to Live (capital L) and Write (capital W)? More than once that summer you had complained that she adored not you but her dream of you. Now the dream had gone – had you begun to recognize that? She had climbed down off her high perch but she couldn't love less than the dream. You knew it would have aroused jealousy and worse if you had managed better with Cecelia Skyways; but did you recognize that it had aroused a little grain of contempt that you had failed?

And could you have believed that among the thousand conflicting feelings that came to her when her mind returned, as it often did, to the scene she had come upon in the outhouse flat, there was a certain admiration, a certain detached appreciation of its visual quality, even a wish to see it performed again, and at the same time a very practical irritation that you hadn't first done the shopping and waved the red towel before getting down to your business with the tail-end of Felice Stockman? You were too indecisive for her, too wavering (two steps forward and one step back) over the sands of your dreaming. You needed, as she told you, ballast in the head. You needed a certain thickening of the skin and coarsening of the nerve fibres. You were a callow youth, Curlyboy, you were destined to be a callow youth all your life, and Aorewa was waking from her dream.

But all this was inward with her and it was not coming out. Until further notice she was going to be plain Pat Bennett carrying inside her a small blending of juices which she wanted extracted before they evolved out of a liquid nothing into a foetal something, and you, Curl Skidmore, were to make the arrangement. And meanwhile life went on as usual in Mrs Battle's white courtyard. Felice sang, a little waveringly, a little nervously, as if keeping up appearances with difficulty, and waved out as if nothing had happened. And Nathan, who so long ago had harboured suspicions of his wife's interest in the young writer from along the beach and then dismissed them when it had proved to be the cook she was after, behaved as if nothing had happened because that was what he believed to be the case. Felice was not going to tell him, and why should Pat? There was nothing to be gained by unsettling him. So Felice and Nathan bounced in their tea-chests and sat on the lids of suitcases as the day of departure got closer, and what was going on inside the sopranohead when it stopped, as it did from time to time, and stared away abstractedly as if it could see through blank walls, was anyone's guess, and you, Curl Skidmore, guessed right, because she was seeing in her mind what you were seeing in yours, and like you she was wishing for more of the same and regretting that it couldn't be.

It was Melior Farbro to whom you went for help. Who else was there? You weren't to know that his cartoons had run to a halt and that although the series had worried him because it seemed so unlike anything he'd done before and so unlike anything he could imagine his friends recognizing as 'serious' art, still it bothered him more that the inspiration should suddenly vanish. He simply couldn't do another, and that made the inspiration itself seem more real, more genuine, and made him regret that it was gone. But you sat, you and he, on either side of the counter between the kitchen and the studio as you had done on that first visit, and Melior gave you lunch and asked how things were going at the university now that the second term had started, and asked had you made up for time lost when you were working at the foundry. You talked about the waterfront dispute and how Sid Holland and his henchman Sullivan were driving the union further and further into a corner, demanding more every time their previous demand was accepted, and while you talked poor Ken Blayburn sat in a chair frowning and saying things silently over to himself. Now and then Melior would toss a remark over to him, raising his voice and speaking very distinctly, and Ken would look up and say, 'Yeah Mel, that's true,' or, 'You're right there Mel,' or, 'I'll say, that'd be corker,' and then he would retire back into his frowning and mouthing. So you got around to the subject you'd come to talk about, Pat's pregnancy, and Melior tut-tutted and winked and laughed all at once, recognizing how serious it was to have an unwanted baby on the way, especially when you weren't married, but at the same time enjoying this proof that his fantasies of the fleshly threshings of his two young friends weren't unfounded. But as to abortion, that was a serious matter, a dangerous game, and Melior rolled himself a careful cigarette and licked it and stuck it down and tweaked out the ends and pushed the makings across to you and lit his and blew a fine stream of grey smoke into the air before he admitted in a very quiet and casual tone that he thought it just possible he might have a friend who knew someone who knew someone, but did Pat understand the risk she was taking? And did she and

Curl know the kind of money these people asked? It would probably cost fifty quid and where would that come from? All his own money, every bean of it, had gone to help Ken and to help get Cecelia Skyways out of the country, and now he thought he would have to have a show of his work but god damn it he would be surprised if his pictures sold and if they did it would be too late for Pat, the tot (you winced, Curl Skidmore, at the thought of a 'tot' in there) would be booting her bellybutton before the money started to come in. So you told him what Pat felt and what she had said, and in the end you told him the whole story, even about Felice, and Melior tut-tutted and smiled and winked, and shook his head and frowned and laughed, and told you you were a double-deceiver and a rotten swine and guffawed so hard he fell off his stool and had to roll himself another cigarette before he could settle down to the business in hand. But he could see from what you told him that Pat had made up her mind, she wasn't going to have that baby. And as for money, you were able to say that some of Nathan's never-to-be-returned loan was available, and you would just bloody well have to find the rest even if it had to come in the form of a loan from your father, the precarious Member for Mt Eden South.

And that's where it did come from, so there was a lunch with the father. It must have been late in June because Parliament had been recalled after five months and the father was clobbered up in his pinstripes and watch-chain and with his free-passage medal for the railways dangling on his paunch, and he was urging you to visit the momma while he was in Wellington, she still got lonely when he was away, and he was worrying about Sid's tactics. At least Labour had a forum now, they could say in Parliament what they wanted to say about the Dispute, but could they count on the papers to report it, and wasn't it too late? After all these months of bombardment from the Press, and over the wireless which Sid had used so unscrupulously, 'the public', which was something real to the father, something whose voice he heard out of the treetops and in the silences of the night, believed it was all as simple as Sid had made it sound.

They believed that unions were controlled by communists and wreckers who were directed from Moscow, and that the war in Korea and on the wharves was the same war, and that Sid and Sullivan had fought it bravely on the home front and were winning, and even that the Government had patiently offered reasonable terms throughout and that the union bosses had rejected them. How long would it take to spell out the whole complicated truth, and where could you do it, and who would be listening by the time you got to the end? Simple stories stuck in the mind and Sid told simple stories. And there was something Sid had said, some kind of off-the-cuff challenge he'd thrown out that made the father suspect he was considering calling an early election on the issue of the Dispute, taking a leaf out of Pig Iron Bob's book in Australia, a ploy which had paid off. Poor precarious Member! How terrified you were of that threat, because you were never wrong in what those voices told you that came down from the treetops and up out of the silences of the night. You always read them right and you knew your seat was precarious and that if Sid called an election now you were out. And you had held Mt Eden South since the felt hat of Ken Blayburn had joined the beret of Melior Farbro in the air outside the Auckland central post office in November 1935. It was yours, as if by right, you had got used to being there and going to and fro on the railway when Parliament was in session, making your always-the-same campaign address about how the Tories had watched New Zealand slide into a depression and how Labour had dragged the country out of it, and wearing your big red rosette and handing out half-crowns on election day to your son and his friends who had delivered your pamphlets and stuck up your posters: 'VOTE LABOUR AGAIN: SKIDMORE FOR MT EDEN SOUTH.' It had become a ritual, safe, dependable, and after each election you climbed again those grey steps into Parliament Buildings in the cold wet Wellington wind with the same sense of pride, of satisfaction, of having made it, that came to you after that never-to-be-equalled election night of 1935. Labour had held office until 1949 and when it lost an election you found it hard to believe and yet it was what 'the public' had been telling you, and at least you'd kept your own seat. But now even the seat didn't seem safe. You didn't quite say so to young Urlich, you didn't say it to anyone, but your son read your anxiety and in his pity for you he refrained from offering all the good advice he'd been saving up for you: that you should go down fighting, that you shouldn't equivocate, that you should speak out and say exactly what you thought and to hell with them. If you were going to lose then at least you should lose with a good grace, Urlich thought; lose with style. It had all sounded fine inside his head, thought out in advance as the ferry made its way across the harbour to town. But here now confronting you over the gloomy lunch table of the Empire Tea Rooms it didn't seem possible even to mention the word defeat. You would win again no matter when Sid called an election, there could be no doubt of it – that's what he told you. The people of Mt Eden South wanted you, you'd done so much for them – and you allowed yourself for the moment to believe it, and smiled, and shut your ears to those voices that were hovering up there singing a little song that went 'Goodbye Skidmore, you've had a good run.' So the subject of money came up late and the father who wanted to help and wanted the son to get his degree from the university and wanted to see him safe and secure in a job that one day might put him in the thousand-a-year class, and wanted to see him respectable, either married to that very lovely girl, or better still, since there seemed to be a lick of the tarbrush there, away from her and on his own – the father said he didn't think he could manage fifty just now but would twenty-five do in the meantime? Out in the street they paused helplessly, neither one knowing how to give vent to the anxiety and pity and love that arose in him when he looked into the eyes of the other, and in the end they parted with a joke or two, a few conventional words, and a rather shy accidental shaking of hands.

And just a little later it must have been, because by then the arrangement with the friend of a friend who knew someone who knew someone had been made, Melior called at the verandah flat and suggested a walk around to Thorne's Bay because it was one of those mild days in winter when the sky clears and the sun comes out and it's difficult to remember what season of the year it really is. And Curl and Pat were both agreeable because the truth was they were uneasy now with one another, they didn't quarrel but their talk was artificial and strained and when Curl spoke to her he felt tension in his throat and heard his voice go up a register beyond what the subject spoken about called for. At night they lay together innocently folded around one another in the big bed, Pat looked for that assurance and always found it, but in the daytime she behaved as if it didn't count, they were estranged. So they walked, the three of them, to Thorne's Bay, and then because it was a good day and the Gulf was so beautiful in the winter sun they went on to Milford. And in those days there was, somewhere along there on the water's edge, a ramshackle tea rooms that also sold fish and chips and because it was late in the afternoon Melior suggested they should have what Ken Blayburn would call 'a feed'. They sat in the verandah room looking out through the dozen paint-peeling windows, right down the vast blue out-reach of the Hauraki Gulf past Rangitoto to the eastern suburbs of Auckland on one side and out beyond Motutapu Island towards the Coromandel peninsula on the other. Melior did all the talking. He told them that when Edward Lear had written:

On the coasts of Coromandel
Where the early pumpkins blow

he hadn't got the name Coromandel from India as everyone supposed but from New Zealand because he had a sister living on the peninsula who must have written saying how well pumpkins grew. And in the poem Melior thought Lear must have written 'grow' and then changed it to 'blow', and what a marvellous Learish change that had been! And Melior told them his own name – or the name his parents had given him – was really Heap, Melvin Heap, and he'd changed it when he was a young man partly because he didn't like the idea of a painting of his (he'd thought very early of posterity, he acknowledged with a wry smile) being referred to as 'a Heap', and partly because he'd wanted a foreign-sounding and slightly preposterous name to match the avant garde paintings he was doing in those days when he travelled to Morocco and then on to Paris. The name had begun half as a joke and then it had stuck and he'd been glad of it (so he said) because with his tastes in sexual matters he felt sure he would end up one day in the courts and he'd thought it would be as well to spare his parents the embarrassment, the social disgrace, that might have followed the publication of his name in the papers. And he told them that he'd now arranged an exhibition of his new work, it was being mounted, and he couldn't help feeling pleased with it even though it had come rather abruptly to a dead stop, but he was sure no one would like it. And he mentioned the date arranged through the friend of a friend who knew someone who knew someone and asked did they have it in mind, and Pat said *she* had it in mind all right, she had it so much in mind there wasn't room there for anything else, so whether it was in Curl's mind or not hardly mattered.

History is always written as if the doings of ordinary nameless faceless persons such as the young unmarried couple looking for a juice extractor were a grey and ill-defined background to the stage on which the politicians strut and strike attitudes and make decisions and laws, but of course history is not reality, it is merely fiction badly written, and in reality it is the other way about, the politicians are the grey background to ordinary lives, however their strutting and posturing and decision- and law-making may bear upon the availability of juice-extractors. So let us put SuperSid, together with Sullivan and Holyoake, with whom he is discussing the possibility of an early election, firmly into the haze of their own cigar smoke and the mumble of their own self-congratulatory platitudes, and focus instead this evening on the gangplank of the Auckland ferrywharf and upon the young couple coming down it, he tall, slim, clean-cut, close-shaven, with neatly brushed fair hair and woven tie, a jacket of harris tweed and flannel trousers of dark grey, she with luxuriantly wavy and glossy black hair in her two-piece suit of grey worsted with padded shoulders and calf-length skirt, and with an embroidered blouse, seamed stockings and high-heeled shoes. Each of them carries over the right arm a neatly folded gabardine raincoat because although the night is mild for this time of year there is the possibility it might rain. They are met at the entrance to the ferry building by Melior's friend of a friend, a middle-aged woman who looks a little flustered and worried but who is kind and reassuring and who says she knows what it is to be pregnant when you don't want to be. She has a car parked nearby and she drives them to a tree-lined street somewhere on the lower slopes of Remuera where they get out and meet the friend's friend who is also a middle-aged woman, also slightly flustered but kind and reassuring, who puts them into her car and tells them as she starts it up and backs down the drive that she knows what it is to be pregnant when you don't want to be. So they drive across the middle part of Auckland, through Parnell, down into the hollow of Queen Street and up the other side into those little streets with wooden houses clustered together which date from the last century and which at this moment, in the first winter of the second half of the twentieth century, are quite unfashionable and running to seed. The friend's friend drives them up on to the ridge of Ponsonby and down into the hollow towards Grey Lynn and there she pulls up outside a large sprawling two-storeyed wooden house that must once have been grand but is so no longer, where she hands them over to the person known to her, another middle-aged lady, rather less 'respectable' but quite as kind, a Mrs Hinchinghorn she might be except that there are no names. And this lady takes them indoors and tells them she knows what it is to be pregnant when you don't want to be and not to be frightened but from now on it will have to be a bit cloak-and-daggerish because you know what the penalties are for doing this kind of job so no one will do it without taking precautions. In a few minutes, this person known to the friend's friend tells them, she is going to take them up the street and leave them on the corner and there they will be met by a person who will ask them is this Clondike Road to which they must reply No it's half past two. And in a few minutes the lady who might be Mrs Hinchinghorn but who is nameless takes them into the street and they go around the corner and across the road and into another smaller darker street and there she leaves them on the corner. It is very dark and Curl Skidmore is cold and his stomach is turning over with fear at what is going to be done to Pat but Pat is firm and quite severe and shows no fear at all. So when another woman approaches them and asks is this Clondike Road it is Pat who replies firmly, 'No it's half past two'. This woman says they are to follow her and even in the dark you can see that she is making the most of her part. She looks from left to right and moves forward in little darting runs, furtive through two further streets and down an alley between two fences of corrugated iron and through a gate into the back garden of a little house where in the dark Curl makes out what looks like a vegetable patch with a few old cabbage heads running to seed. They go inside and the woman who is leading them switches on a light and suggests they sit down. She is probably the same age as the other women but so glaringly brightly made up she looks like a stage clown or a scarecrow, with wispy dyed hair on top through which the light shows broad gaps like tracks through a forest. She sits down on a hideous mottled couch away from which three China ducks are attempting to escape up the wall, and she hands them cigarettes and lights one herself and is immediately convulsed with a coughing spasm that lasts the best part of a minute. That over she doesn't tell them she knows what it is to be pregnant when you don't want to be. She tells them 'he' will be here soon, that it isn't her house, they merely have the use of it, and is there anything they want to ask before they hand over the fifty – and she hopes they brought it in used singles as instructed. Pat and Curl both speak at once, they have each been worrying, Pat wanting to know how she can be sure whatever they do will work, Curl wanting to know is it likely to leave her sterile. Both these questions set the painted lady laughing which in turn stirs up her cough but the answer to both when it comes is the same. It works all right, and it doesn't stop you getting pregnant again. Half the shop-girls in Karangahape Road have been through her hands (it's the expression she uses) and most of them are back for a second go before they start to learn some sense. Pat has shown no sign of nervousness but she asks now will it hurt and the painted crone is glad of this question, she smiles receiving it and is happy to deliver her prepared answer, that when you pick a ripe apple it comes away easily but if you pick it green you have to pull. This is so horrifying to Curl Skidmore he feels the blood drain from his face and he has to bend over in his chair pretending to tie a shoelace for fear of fainting. But now 'he' can be heard in the next room, and at a knock on the wall the painted crone, who has been passing the time counting the fifty used single pound notes they have handed her gets up and ties a blindfold around Pat's eyes. 'Just a little precaution,' she says; and signalling to Curl to stay right where he is, she leads Pat into the next room, closing the door behind her. No father-to-be, let it be said, paces the floor more anxiously than a father-not-to-be, and Curl Skidmore has no great space in which to stretch his long legs, but the ever-escaping China ducks see him passing to and fro the length of the couch and a little to spare at either end forty times, fifty, one for each year of the century and on into the eighties perhaps before there is any sound or signal from the next room. The ducks are beginning to get used to him, but still bent on flying away from that couch which looks like a huge padded mouth wide open and ready to shut on anything that sits in it, when the crone with the forest-walks through her dyed hair returns to say 'he' is packing up and the young lady will be ready in a moment. And when Pat appears, removing the blindfold, she looks a little pale and shaky but none the worse for it. The crone says she's sorry she can't make them a cup of tea but there will be a taxi waiting for them on the corner in five minutes. She leads them out by the back way again, turning off the lights as she goes, out into the back garden, through the gate in the iron fence and along the alley, down the road and down another road, possibly needlessly around a block to confuse them, and there on the corner she leaves them telling them to wait and the taxi will come soon. 'Have some towels ready, it should start to work in a couple of hours,' she says, and it's only then Curl Skidmore understands that whatever has to come out is still in there and that it's not all over yet. And now they look in pockets and purse and find they haven't the fare for a taxi and they have to hurry away before it comes. They go in the direction they think will take them to where the trams run. Pat is feeling wobbly but they hurry nevertheless. When they stop to rest Pat supports herself against a fence but it is Curl who is sick in the gutter.

Tram, ferry, bus – all the shaky way home they are worrying because Pat says she felt very little, no dilation ('At your cervix Madame, you'll be dilated,' had been Melior's joke), no knitting needle, no puncture, only something in there, an instrument, a certain amount of pressure but no pain, and then an injection of some fluid and a smell of chlorine. Has anything happened, or have they been tricked out of fifty pounds? But as they get ready for bed Pat reports that the bleeding has started. She settles down beside him padded with towels.

'And all are false that taste not just like mine.' So much the poet Donne claims for his tears of true love, and so much we claim for the scene which follows. Accept no imitations (there are some). This is the real story. As you will see we have gone to the only available source for the truth. So here is Takapuna beach empty at perhaps 2 a.m. and here is Curl Skidmore carrying a soaked towel and a bowl of blood. Could we just check on that Curl.

It was a bowl of blood?

It was an old po lent me for the occasion by Nathan Stockman. He used it for friars balsam. For inhalations. He suffered from catarrh. It was horribly brown stained with balsam . . .

So we see Curl Skidmore in his pyjamas and dressing gown carrying a large ornate brown-stained chipped china bowl full . . . Was it full?

I don't remember. Half full perhaps. There was a lot of blood.

Down to the sea. Why would that be when across the yard in the outhouse there was a lavatory?

There was no light in the lavatory and we shared it with Nathan and Felice. I was afraid of splashing it about.

So Curl Skidmore carries the bowl across the lawn, down the

steps under the tamarisk feathers, over the sand and down to the shallows. It is one of those nights with high-flying spaced-out clouds and a big moon and when he looks up the moon appears to be racing through static fleeces which it lights up as it goes. He is full of some unresolved and swelling emotion, part fear, part horror, part guilt.

Look here, aren't you laying it on?

Is that not what you felt?

I was prone to melodrama.

So you didn't, as reported, feel a sense of sin?

How do we know what we feel? We find words for what we think we feel and that puts a limit on it. Perhaps falsifies . . .

Thank you for that reminder. But you will see we haven't yet got the blood into the water. We have you in pyjamas and dressing gown and we have the blood in the stained china jerry and we have the moon travelling light up there and we have you feeling – something. What was it?

All you've said and more. Love, Guilt, Ecstasy, Fear – anything you like. It was a big moment in my life. I was a father-to-be for the first time and now I was a father-not-to-be, and in the bowl was the child-not-to-be of Curl and Pat. I tipped the blood into the sea and I thought of the German momma and the Anglo-Saxon Kiwi father and the Tuhoe forebears and the de Thierry forebears and even the godamn dark Celts – it was a powerful mix I was throwing away. And up there was the moon and out there was Rangitoto. I was afraid.

Afraid of what?

That the gods might punish I suppose.

And did Pat feel . . .

Pat was a practical girl. She said, 'My Tuhoe forebears practised infanticide. So did yours probably.'

So now you have rolled your pyjamas up to the knees and you are barefoot in the shallows. You are tipping the bowl of blood into the sea. You think of Macbeth and the multitudinous seas incarnadine. In one of those flash floods of moonlight when the clouds are travelling fast you see the dark stain in the water, you see it spreading, you watch it fade. There is no other witness . . .

There was one.

Someone else was there?

Hiroshima, *mon ami*.

Ah, the little dog. Rosh.

He sometimes slipped his chain at night and went roaming. He wanted me to throw a stick. I wasn't in the mood for it. He jumped up and pulled at the tassel on my dressing gown. I whacked him on the nose and he ran off whimpering. It was the only time I ever hit him. I called him but he wouldn't come back . . .

So the bowl is empty. There's still the towel. It's soaked through with blood. You try to rinse it and wring it out in the shallows but it's hopelessly sodden and in the end you simply swing it and throw it as far as you can. The tide is on its way out and will take it out to sea. Back in the bedroom Pat reports she thinks the flow is easing. She pads herself some more and you settle down on towels to sleep.

But the flow wasn't easing. In the morning the towels were soaked through, the mattress was sodden, Pat was pale, whether with fright or loss of blood. Curl was paler without loss of any blood at all but in the matter of pallor he had a head start. He was quick on his feet however, and he panted up the steep drive and through the early morning streets to the phone box and had an ambulance there in – well, however long it took. Pat was driven to Devonport in time to cross on an early vehicular crossing and she was already anaesthetized and being spooned out on a table in a theatre of National Women's Hospital before the tide which had carried away the dream that was to be called Siegfried or Sieglinde had returned uncarnadined.

She was none the worse for it. She was fit as a flea – a box of birds. The doctor's reassurances made Curl feel he could breathe freely and he silently put up with what followed about not getting girls pregnant if you didn't intend to marry them and not taking advantage of a girl's racial origins and what a beautiful girl she was anyway, there weren't many pakeha girls could hold a candle to her . . .

He found her dozing, the anaesthetic had left her sleepy, but she woke immediately and liked the flowers and the fruit and the book and told him she would be out in the morning. She didn't like this place, she didn't like the way they treated her, the special tone they adopted, as if they were being especially good about the fact she wasn't married and had almost certainly (although she hadn't admitted it) been to a back-street abortionist before coming to them. But she was pleased she'd done it – she felt such relief, such a huge load had been taken off her, such a dark shadow had sailed away, and now she was thinking about the future. There were so many things she wanted to do, and she'd been listening to Rex Fairburn and John Weeks lately talking about London and the Slade School and she thought that's where she would like to go. And Curl held her hand and listened for something that ought to be there just under the surface of what she was saying, sat still, listening, strained to hear it, as you might strain to hear a heart beat. He was trying to discover whether these plans for the future included him, and though there was nothing in what she said that suggested they did there was nothing that seemed to rule him out either. She talked of Jim and June going, and Cecelia, and now it was Nathan and Felice and at that she remembered what day it was and asked did he have it in mind, and he pretended that he did, that he hadn't forgotten, that he'd planned all along to go straight from visiting her to the wharves to see off Nathan and Felice who were sailing that afternoon. And she closed her eyes, sleepy again, and he sat holding her hand and looking at her beautiful face, and then for a minute or two his eyes closed too and he slept sitting beside the bed.

There was a big circle of the Stockmans' friends and relations in the lounge on A deck of the *Ruahine*, the sister ship of the *Rangitane* in which Cecelia had sailed. There were a lot of Nathan's relatives and a few of Felice's and a lot of others who were musicians and somehow they'd all managed to get passes to come on board and they were sitting in a circle around the departing pair talking, most of them, in those very clear loud voices musical people have, exchanging jokes and dissolving into gales of laughter. They had all heard earlier in the day that the wharfies' National Executive had voted to go back to work on the Government's terms, the dispute was over, they were defeated, and now someone brought the news that Sid had dissolved Parliament and called a General Election on the issue of the Strike, and there were groans and cries of dismay and everyone was sure Sid would win, that he'd out-manoeuvred Labour, the 1949 election would be ratified and this was really the end of the good years for New Zealand. The voices and the laughter got louder but there was an edge of despair in it, or so Curl Skidmore thought, and friends were saying to Nathan and Felice keep a space for us on your floor in London, we'll be coming too before much longer. Curl had his eyes on Felice and for a long time she seemed not to notice him at all, or to avoid his eye, but then all at once in the thick of the noise she looked straight across at him and winked.

You didn't stay, Urlich Ambrose, for the streamers and the last rites as the ship sailed. There were enough there to do that, one more or less wouldn't make any difference, and that wink was the last communication that ever passed between you and the extraordinary Felice. But you did see her once more. It must have been fifteen years later, you were in London on sabbatical leave, and someone gave you a ticket for one of the operas in Wagner's Ring Cycle at Covent Garden. It started at six thirty and you got there at the last minute and didn't have time to buy a programme. The soprano who sang Brunnhilde was short and overweight but with an electrifying voice, and right from the start there was something familiar about her, about the voice itself, but it was a movement of the hand and a turn of the head that gave her away. Her girth had grown with her voice, and her reputation with both, and now all three were outsize, and as she made her way singing down the mountainside ringed with fire from which the Siegfried had released her, it was difficult to connect that rotundity in cardboard armour with the lively little sexual activist in Mrs Battle's outhouse flat. But as you listened to her singing there was no mistaking it. It was the Felicevoice, the same that in the little white yard with the cabbage tree at its centre had gone up and down in the role of Grimgerde or some minor Valkyrie – the same Felicevoice, but now enhanced, augmented, liberated, expanded; and at the end yours was one of the first and the loudest of the cheers that went up.

And now the ship has sailed, the Gulf is empty, the sun is going down, and Curl Skidmore is sitting at the window looking out to the beach and thinking he will do himself grilled bacon and a tin of baked beans. Something in the small waves lapping the beach catches his eye, something white that twists and curls and rolls and vanishes and reappears. He goes down the steps into the yard, through the trellis gate across the lawn, down the steps and across the sand, and there it is, whiter than the whitest wash, clean and unstained, returned by the laundering tide – the towel so hopelessly blood-sodden the night before when he had delivered it, for ever so he thought, to the deep.

NINE

A Good Run

The tides flow in and out, regular as clockwork and mysteriously complicated in their awkward matchings with the hours of the day. There are probably some winter winds, certainly some rain, and possibly some days when the sky clears and the sun shines and you begin to think it won't be too long before you're swimming again. Nathan and Felice sailed six weeks ago and must have reached London. Melior's show has been arranged, the pictures which you still haven't been allowed to see have been mounted, the publicity has gone out and the opening is due soon. Pat has long since recovered and now the August vacation is here she has gone north to be with her parents. She has taken most of her things with her to make it easier for you to accomplish the transfer across the yard to the outhouse flat which you have decided to take because it's cheaper than the verandah flat. The snap Election Sid Holland has called on the issue of the waterfront dispute is being fought and your hopes rise continually against the warnings of reason that there's no chance of a Labour victory.

We put these facts before you, Urlich Ambrose, to help you get your bearings because this was a confusing time for you, a period when you were more than ever prone to lose things and forget times and dates. So it was now late in August and you were coming down Queen Street on the left hand side, crossing Wellesley Street from the Civic Theatre. There was a green-painted wooden two-storeyed signal box there to watch over the intersection where the trams seemed to need help from outside to make their right or left turns out of or into the main street. And you remember being there because you ran into a student, not a close friend but one whose name you recall easily because it was Harry Truman. And he told you he hadn't heard you weren't living at home and he'd phoned to ask something about the third term timetable and the father had answered and when your friend said, 'It's Harry Truman here,' the father had replied, 'Good, and this is Douglas MacArthur.' So you thought the father hadn't lost his sense of humour and you felt guilty because he was fighting an election campaign and you hadn't been home to visit and hadn't ranged yourself at any of his meetings along with the momma and the sisters so he could show you all off and show that he was head of a united family. You'd let yourself off the trienniel torture of the father's campaign speech, addressed so often to the bristling backs of empty chairs, about how the Tories had let the country slide down the drain and Labour had pulled it up again. You knew he would be avoiding the issue Sid had nominated, the waterfront dispute. You knew he would be afraid to commit himself to an unpopular line, and you couldn't bear to watch him losing in a cowardly fashion. But you were cowardly yourself not giving him support, and you knew it, because you knew, not literally but in the way sons know about their fathers and fathers know about their sons, that he would be hearing those deadly voices out of the treetops and in the silences of the night singing, 'Goodbye Skidmore, you've had a good run,' and you felt sorry for him and hopeless about him and that's why you remember not only the student's name but what he said to you. But of course you had followed the campaign, every move of it, and maybe the biggest thing in it for you was the thought that if it went even moderately well so Labour just held its own, the father would be back in Mt Eden South. And in fact when you met the student Harry Truman you were coming down from the Town Hall where you'd listened to Sid Holland winding up his northern campaign and you'd heckled him about the cost of the Dispute to the country. 'Forty-two million,' you shouted, and Sid shouted back that that was communist propaganda. Was the Government statistician a communist you shouted, and Sid replied that it wasn't the forty-two million that was propaganda, it was communist propaganda that it was his government that had cost the country that money. It was the watersiders who'd cost the country forty-two million – they and their communist masters who pulled the strings, and their stooges like our young friend down there who needs a shave. And he'd roused a cheer at that and when you tried to heckle again he kept his mouth very close to the microphone and shouted to drown you out.

So we have you in Queen Street, Curl Skidmore, talking to the student Harry Truman and he asks are you growing a beard and you put your hand up to your face, remembering Sid's description of you as needing a shave, and discover there's a stubble all over it. It's days since you've shaved but you haven't remembered and haven't noticed the growth. You suggest a cup of coffee at Somervell's which is the intellectual coffee bar where poets and painters and people from the university go, and as you walk in and find yourselves a place you see Rex Fairburn a few tables away and he remembers you from the reading at Nathan Stockman's house and he calls out in his big booming voice, 'Here's that Skidmore lad, don't let him read, he'll set the place on fire.' And a few minutes later he stops at your table on his way out and asks how you're doing and what have you been writing and how far have you got with those two novels and how's poor Nathan Stockman been since his place burned down and is it true the Insurance wouldn't pay out and are you growing a beard. He doesn't wait for answers to all of these questions because all at once he thinks to ask the time and Harry Truman tells him, and Rex says he'd better hop along up the hill because he's on his way to Farbro's opening and he's supposed to be making a speech. You are glad of that exchange because Melior's exhibition has gone right out of your mind, so in a few minutes we have you leaving Harry Truman at Somervell's and following the path Rex Fairburn has taken, climbing Wellesley Street into Symonds Street where a little path runs down beside a building that might be a block of flats and at the back is the gallery where Melior's paintings are on display.

Everything was confusing for you at that time so you grew

bristles as fast as winter weeds sprouted up through the raked clearing that had been Cecelia Skyways' Zen garden and it took Sid Holland and Harry Truman and Rex Fairburn to make you aware of them. But there's no need to remind you of Melior's show. You remember it because of the force with which it struck you. And perhaps you remember it too because you've dined out on the story so often. These were not, as Melior had seemed to hint, just elaborate jokes. Cartoons they might be, in the strictest sense, but they were not comic strip cartoons. It's true they were human figures, part caricatures of real people, and with speech balloons. But they were marvellous bold colours, they were forms in movement, and even the balloon words floated and soared and sailed like kites in their lurid skies. You were exhilarated, Curl Skidmore, and you said so to Melior who laughed and was pleased, but he took you by the shoulder and said, 'Have a look around, boy,' and then you saw what he meant. Almost every face was puzzled, there were frowns, there were looks of embarrassment, this wasn't what they expected of the old master, and there were no red stickers on the wall. 'You'd better pick out a couple you like,' Melior said, 'and you can have them when the show's over. No one's going to buy.'

It wasn't quite as bad as that but only a few sold, and the next day the *Herald*'s art critic headed his column, 'Not the New Zealand we all Know and Love,' and the *Star*'s was headed, 'Puzzling New Work by Melior Farbro.' Fewer than half of that series survive and there's a problem of preservation because they were done on heavy paper and should have been framed under glass but Farbro mounted them down on board because it was all he could afford. And of course it's well remembered by people who visited Farbro during his last lonely years how when the curtains on his studio windows rotted and fell into shreds he used to prop against the glass bits of hardboard with the cartoons still attached, but lifting at the corners and bubbling in the middle, to keep the sun off his day bed. Two of the most admired of the series, and certainly the best preserved, are the two which adorn the white stucco wall with the clerestory light of Professor Urlich Skidmore's Parnell townhouse, and which were given to the professor at the time when he still had ambitions to be a writer. On another wall in the same room hangs an Aorewa de Thierry, a cubist piece of two lovers against a sea-wall which is generally agreed to be student work and derivative, but full of remarkable promise.

That was in the week before the election and you were expecting Patagonia back that weekend because the Saturday was the first day of September and lectures for third term were to start on the Monday. You had the outhouse flat clean and tidy, you had your clothes in three drawers of the chest of drawers and half of the wardrobe, with the other four drawers and the remaining half of the wardrobe dusted and ready for hers. You had got a man to come and take away the blood-stained mattress and you'd bought a lumpy second-hand one to replace it, and you'd heaved your furniture across the yard and set up the yellow table with the tablegram on it and the lamp with the Japanese design on its shade. The other table where you ate your meals you put at the window looking out to sea as it had done in the verandah flat. You even took that beautiful matting, which came from the islands in those days around cases of bananas and could be bought for a few shillings, down from the weatherboard wall of the verandah flat and tacked it up in the outhouse flat, edging it with batons of half-round and hanging at its centre the picture in which you and she were forever cubed together in the night against the sea-wall. The work was finished on Saturday and that was election day and you waited all day for her but she didn't come and late in the afternoon you went out and cast a vote for Labour which was the first vote you'd ever cast because you'd only recently turned twenty-one. You spent the day reading and playing records – those old 78s of Beniamino Gigli singing 'La Donna e Mobile' and 'Salve Dimora casta e pura', and the 'Eine Kleine Nacht' music on four sides of 45s, one side for each movement, and some of the Beethoven piano sonatas on 78s that had done heavy duty, and of course the Wagnermusic, which had so stirred you all after the cake that day in summer, and which seemed now so full of grief and pain and menace. And as the day wore on you got more and more nervous because you were worrying about the

142

election result or because Pat hadn't turned up. It seemed it was Pat's absence that worried you most but there was no reason for that because she hadn't said when she would be back, it was just that you had fixed your mind on Saturday and you still felt it had to be the day. You made pan-fried rice and oysters, enough for you both, and as the first election results came over the radio and she hadn't come you began to eat it, meaning to leave half in case she should arrive later in the evening, but in your nervousness you ate it all. It wasn't long before it began to be obvious that Sid Holland was going to win, that he would probably increase his majority, and then all your hopes hung on the result in Mt Eden South and it was going to be close, it swung this way and that as the results came in from the polling booths, and you kept waiting for the count from the booth at the little school with the motto IT IS TONE THAT MAKES MUSIC which was said always to declare which way the result would finally go. Between the broadcasts of results you walked up and down the beach and along the sand to the rocks and back because you couldn't keep still and each time you crossed the lawn you could see Mrs Battle and Charles in their front room totting up results and once as you came up from the beach the french doors were open and Mrs Battle was sitting up in her chair clapping and out in the shadow of the verandah, but lit up as he passed the windows, Clipper Charles in his eagle shirt was marching up and down hitting a saucepan with a spoon. That was at half past ten or eleven and it was all over, Sid had won. He'd taken four more seats from Labour and one of them was Mt Eden South. Let's not pretend that you did much sleeping that night, but you did a lot of walking up and down the beach reciting to the moon the names of Pat and Cleopatra and Patagonia, and Siegfried and Sieglinde, and Aorewa who was also de Thierry, and Cecelia who was also Dawn, and Felice who was always and only Felice, while somewhere in the heavens over and beyond Rangitoto, and in the airwaves, and in the workings of colour and action that were the cartoons of Melior Farbro, Sidney George Holland thanked his stars and his people that he was once again their chosen one, and that his vision was theirs of a time when tennis clubs and barber shops would glitter over the

143

land, when babies would be delivered by storks and found under cabbage bushes, when a Girl Guide salute would signify cleanliness of body and mind and a worker would know better than to ask for five and twopence when his master was offering four and tenpence ha'penny.

And 'Oh Early,' said the momma when her boy rang next morning, 'how you haf neglected us.' She made him feel that the father's loss of Mt Eden South was because the son had not visited them during the campaign, because he was too selfish, too absorbed in his own affairs, which in turn was because he was not sufficiently fortified by the momma's cakes and because he had not been taking his vitamin C. But the father only said Oh well he'd had a good run, and his voice seemed to come up from the bottom of a well.

So Sunday vanished into a hole and on Monday lectures began and you phoned the Elam School of Art and called there in the early afternoon but no one had seen Pat Bennett or heard from her. But that evening Mrs Battle step-dragged and 'Gurr-l'ed into and across the yard with a letter that you could see at a glance was from Pat and in order to drive her away so you could read it you told her when she began to crow about the election that you'd heard on the bus coming home that Sid Holland had had a heart attack and died and she said Oh no she couldn't believe that, you were pulling her leg, but she wasn't quite sure that you were and it sent her step-dragging and gasping into retreat, stopping a moment in the middle of the yard to hold on to the cabbage tree and regain her breath, and by that time you had already opened the letter and you were reading and reading again, 'Earlybird and Curlyboy sorry your sovran lady hasn't been in touch but look, darling, there's something to be explained so will you be at Melior's on Tuesday about 1.30 and I'll phone you there? Can't say more now but don't worry. Love, de T.'

Don't worry she said, and she said something to be explained, and darling she said and your sovran lady. And she said

Earlybird and she said Curlyboy and she said cantsaymorenow and she said I'llphoneyouthere. And then Love she said, and she signed it not Pat nor Patagonia nor Cleopatra, not Aorewa either, but the most dangerous of all, de T. And don't worry she said. And she said don't worry. So we will leave a gap to represent Curl Skidmore, Urlich Ambrose, third year third term 1951 student in the Faculty of Arts at the Auckland University College, waking and sleeping (a lot of waking, a little sleep) notworrying himself sick for eighteen hours.

Now we have brought you full circle or back where we began at Melior Farbro's board and it is some time after 1 p.m. and there is the same tea towel with the same brown checks on which Melior dries his spatulate fingers, and Melior is limping about on the kitchen side of the counter making a lunch he suspects young Skidmore won't eat and making soothing noises about Pat saying she'll be back and if it had been anything serious she wouldn't have written that note. And he tells Curl how he, Melior, worried about little Kenny and thought he would never be right again but look at him now – and he takes Curl to the window at the back and there in the garden wearing a felt hat and digging a patch for early spring planting is Ken Blayburn watched by Rosh who is sitting quite close, and watched from a distance by the cats Agatha and Christie who are sitting just inside the open door of Cecelia Skyways' hut which Ken now occupies. And on the camp bed in there you can see Best Bets, and the *Herald* open at the racing page, and on the chair there is a sweater and some tobacco, and on the floor some underclothes and socks. Ken is digging long straight rows deep into the rich black composted soil and his face is calm, he no longer mutters to himself or frowns. His rows encroach on what used to be Cecelia Skyways' Zen garden where already the raked swirling sea-patterns have vanished under weeds but the scoria stones still float like islands, and for a moment Curl remembers the summer and the garden seems to fill again with the sound of her typewriter and with the flying words of her *Memoirs of a Railway Siding*.

'He's right as rain,' Melior says of Ken. 'I'll soon be wishing he was silly in the head again. He'll be off to town and I'll be sitting here listening for the last bus and when he comes home I'll give him a roasting and he'll punish me by telling me what he's been up to.' And Melior puts an arm lightly around Curl's thin shoulders. 'In this love business, boy, things are never just what you want – not for more than a day or two in a decade, I reckon.' And the phone rings.

You had him blocked every way, Patagonia. You were phoning from Princes Wharf, you'd said goodbye to your parents up north and there was just your sister keeping watch for you at the gangway. Your luggage was aboard, you'd found your cabin, the ship was to sail at two and you'd come ashore just to make this phone call. It had to be short. Of course he wanted to come and talk to you, to wave to you, but you pointed out that the next ferry was at 1.45 and there wasn't much chance he'd catch it and even if he did he would only see your ship sailing out as his ferry sailed in. And he wanted you to get your luggage off and come back to him. And he wanted you to hold up the ship and wait for him to join it. And he said he would be following on the very next ship. And he said he would never speak or write to you again. And he said he would swim out after the ship and keep swimming until he drowned. And he said you were a bitch. And he said he loved you and he would never love anyone else. And he pleaded and threatened and cajoled and bargained and wept and shouted and whispered but you stuck to it, Aorewa, you were sure it was for the best, it was best for him as well as for you, and anyway it couldn't be undone. That was why you'd arranged it like this, so it couldn't be changed, so he couldn't weaken your resolve, so neither fear of his threats nor pity for him nor the force of his reasoning would undermine what you'd planned. You were going to London, you were going to study at the Slade School of Art, and although you hadn't finished your diploma at Elam, John Weeks and Rex Fairburn had both written letters saying you'd learned all Elam could teach you and you needed to move on, and they were sure those letters would get you into the Slade. And you had to leave now, because in a very short time the English academic year would be starting. You would be a little late as it was but if you left now you wouldn't be too late to be admitted – and together with the letters from Weeks and from Fairburn had gone sheafs of your work. So if you didn't get in that first time, well, there were other possibilities had been suggested and you would try again the following year. And as for Curl's threat to follow on the very next ship – you were ready for that. He was in the third term of his third year, he must complete his BA and if he didn't – if he came to London without it – you would never consent to see him. He could write to you c/o New Zealand House in the Strand but you would want evidence that he'd completed a BA before you would make any arrangement to see him. And you thought he should think very carefully before following you. He should do an MA and think about things as you would be doing and then maybe in a year or two years the two of you would feel you wanted to meet and start all over again and maybe not. There was plenty of time and there was plenty of space. It was 1951 and there was all the time in the world. And there was the world. Somehow you managed to say all this, de Thierry, between his surges of hysteria and anger and grief, though you weren't sure how much of it he listened to, and you wrote it all again in a long letter which came to him later from Curacao. There was one thing you didn't manage to say on the phone because there wasn't time, and your sister was coming and going from the gangway reporting how close it was getting to the moment when the ship sailed; but you did manage to say it in that one last letter from Curacao. It was that you'd taken a sentimental journey on the service-car north from Kaitaia that goes along the sand at low tide up Ninety Mile Beach and comes back along the rutted road – all the way up the isthmus to Cape Reinga where New Zealand comes to an end and where your Tuhoe forebears say the spirits of our dead fly off to their home. And you sat on the pinnacle of rock there with the satisfying feeling that here was your country coming to an end, narrowing to a point and stopping, and with nothing out there in any direction, nothing but a few reefs and atolls for at least twelve hundred miles, but because of the way the two oceans swirl to meet one another at that point from either side of the island you had the sense already of a bow-wave, that the island was sailing, that the whole country was at your back and before you the open ocean, and you thought of all the ones who had left, and that you were leaving, and you thought someone must stay it will have to be Early. By now you could almost hear his tears splashing into the mouthpiece and your sister was tugging at your sleeve and still he wouldn't release you. 'Please,' you said. 'Early, I've got to go – please say goodbye to me. Please wish me well,' – and he did, and for a moment it destroyed your resolve, because you hadn't expected it. He said, stammered it out, that he wished you well, he wished you every good thing because that was what you deserved, and he said goodbye, and you stood there stunned, your own eyes swimming, and it was your sister who took the phone out of your hand and said, 'She's got to go now, whoever you are. Ta ta. Bye now,' and hung up.

What could Melior do? He'd tried not to listen but the phone was right there by the counter and anyway he wanted to hear what was going on, and when Curl hung up Melior was standing not pretending he hadn't listened, twisting the brown checked tea towel in his hands and looking so sad Curl could see there was no need to explain.

'She's gone,' he said, and they stared at one another, there didn't seem anything to be done, and then Curl asked how long it took a ship to get from Princes Wharf to be off Takapuna beach and Melior said he thought fifteen or twenty minutes and Curl was off running.

You remember the bread smell at Hall's corner, the smell of the bakery there, and the way the blood drummed in your head to the rhythm of 'Goodbye Skidmore, you've had a good run.' Somewhere along there you stopped and bent double because you had run too fast for such a distance and you couldn't keep it up. And Melior had said fifteen or twenty minutes so there was time. But in a minute you were moving again, half-running, half-walking, a sort of unromantic scout's pace, and then at last there was the long steep drive, downhill all the way into the little white courtyard, through the trellis gate, across the lawn and down the steps under the tamarisks, and there was the ship, you were in plenty of time, it was well into the Gulf and coming down the shoreline of Rangitoto but it wasn't yet off Takapuna. So you had time to recover your breath and then as it got nearer you began to pick out details, first the deck cranes and rigging, then the portholes, then the shapes of passengers still out on deck taking their last look at Auckland. And if you could see them, however small they appeared, there was no doubt they could see you there on the empty beach, and it wasn't imaginable that Pat wouldn't be somewhere among them picking out the beach, as Cecelia Skyways had done, and the landmarks of headlands and trees, and finally the white house with the white outhouses. And it was then you thought of the red towel. You'd noticed in making the transfer from the verandah flat it was almost the only thing of Pat's she hadn't taken with her. In a moment you were up and over the lawn and through the window, the nearest, through which Felice had drawn you that rainy morning – then out again and back to the beach. And still the ship wasn't straight off when you unfurled the big red beach towel and flapped it and let it hang out straight and held it high against the background of the white house and walked right down the sand with it into the shallows to be as near as possible. Now the ship was straight off, it was hiding the lighthouse on Rangitoto that looked like a striped pepper grinder, the pepper grinder was emerging on the other side of it, you could measure by that that its speed was increasing and you ran into the water shouting and waving the towel over your head but the ship sailed remorselessly on while you ran with it still waving the red towel. You ran along the beach to the reef and up on to the rocks which were uncovered because the tide wasn't full and there was that fish-head and seaweed smell and the noise of the sea was louder, not of big waves but of many small undisciplined waves slapping and breaking this way and that like voices from a school playground. You scrambled up and over the rocks, over the seaweed grape-clusters, past pools where anemones lay open and little shadows flitted from corner to corner, over the white shining surfaces of raided oyster shells, still waving, still shouting though you knew you couldn't be heard. Did she see you, had she seen the red towel below the white house, had she watched the mad scampering figure running and waving it over the sand and up on to the reef? How could she not have looked for Mrs Battle's house, and looking, how could she not have seen? You stood on the reef and now the ship's angle had altered slightly, it was past Rangitoto and it was heading out as they all did through the gateway to the world. Everywhere else you looked in the Gulf there was the mainland, or islands, or the Coromandel peninsula, but out there through that wide gateway was clear horizon and it was out there the ship was heading. It edged a little to port and now it had its back to you, Curl Skidmore, and soon it seemed not to move but simply to sit on that horizon, to sit there growing smaller. But at the same time it was catching the afternoon light which picked out its white superstructure so it stood there tall and narrow and very clear, but diminishing, a white ship, a white shape, a point of light, a blurr, and nothing at all.

Did she watch, did she see? Inconceivable that she didn't but she rebuts all questions sent out to her into the silences she now inhabits, as she has ignored all letters. You are a lady, Aorewa, who knows when to call it a day, and if I write it is only to assure you Curl Skidmore waved the red towel.

Please visit the Harvill Press website at

www.harvill.com